WILLIAM NAGLE was born in Bacchus Marsh, Victoria, in 1947. Educated at St Joseph's College in Geelong, he left school at seventeen and enlisted in the army. He trained as a cook and in 1966 was deployed with the SAS to Saigon. There he was disciplined for refusing to cook egg custard and later was transferred to the infantry in Australia.

Nagle was discharged from the army in 1968, and went on to work in television, and on stage with the Melbourne Theatre Company. *The Odd Angry Shot*, his debut novel, fictionalised his experiences—and those of his SAS mates—in Vietnam. Nagle completed the first draft in one sitting, working around the clock for six days.

Published in 1975, the novel won the National Book Council Award and became an instant classic. In 1979 it was made into a film starring Graham Kennedy, John Hargreaves, John Jarratt and Bryan Brown. 'It was a risky commercial venture,' said director Tom Jeffrey. 'The Vietnam War was a dirty subject. Few people wanted to be reminded of our involvement.'

Nagle wrote the screenplay for *Death of a Soldier* (1986) and co-wrote the screenplay for *The Siege of Firebase Gloria* (1989), both about the Vietnam War. He worked in film and television for many years in the United States before his death, in 2002.

PAUL HAM's latest book, *Sandakan*, was published by Random House in 2012. He is the author of *Vietnam: The Australian War*, *Kokoda* and *Hiroshima Nagasaki*, published by HarperCollins.

The Odd Angry Shot
William Nagle

Text Publishing Melbourne Australia

textclassics.com.au
textpublishing.com.au

The Text Publishing Company
Swann House
22 William Street
Melbourne Victoria 3000
Australia

First published by Angus & Robertson Publishers, Australia 1975
This edition published by The Text Publishing Company 2013

Cover design by WH Chong
Page design by Text
Typeset by Imogen Stubbs

Printed in Australia by Griffin Press, an Accredited ISO AS/NZS 14001:2004 Environmental Management System printer

Primary print ISBN: 9781922079718
Ebook ISBN: 9781922148087
Author: Nagle, William.
Title: The Odd Angry Shot / by William Nagle;
introduction by Paul Ham.
Series: Text classics.
Other Authors/Contributors: Ham, Paul.
Dewey Number: A823.3

CONTENTS

A Lower Circle of Hell
by Paul Ham

PITY him at your peril. The typical Vietnam veteran—
if any may be called 'typical'—seems to prefer your anger
to your sympathy. To oppose him is to respect him; in
his mind, sympathy and respect are mutually exclusive.
And that is why so many people fail to understand
these men. The Vietnam veteran risked life and limb in
the line of duty—surely that demands our respect? But
on his return from the battlefields of South Vietnam
he got little: mostly contempt, ridicule or, worse, indif-
ference. Hence the rage that burns inside him.

If you doubt this, join one of the veterans' chat
rooms: it is the verbal equivalent of a body blow. Bullying
on Twitter is gentle chiding, by comparison: *Give me a
fight, or give me nothing*, the veterans' collective rant
seems to howl. *Feed my self-loathing, my morbid self-
absorption. 'Cos I'm fucked up and on the loose.*

Many are indeed fucked up. I've interviewed hundreds. Vietnam veterans were the first soldiers to be diagnosed as medically damaged as a *direct consequence* of their exposure to war. In Australia, decades after the fall of Saigon, about thirteen thousand continue to describe themselves as Totally and Permanently Incapacitated.

They are sick. Yet their abnormal state is a response to abnormal conditions: the good news is that to face a violent death, or kill another human being, is not, in fact, normal. The condition has been around since the first Homo sapiens raised a club against another. Rape victims suffer from it, as do witnesses to murder. In Shakespeare's *Henry IV, Part I* Hotspur's wife observes it in her husband, whose sweaty thrashing about in his sleep she compares with 'bubbles in a late disturbed stream'.

Shell shock was the Great War's grisly contribution to the roll call of the afflicted, in the blanked eyes of the first young soldiers to be ordered to march into modern artillery. Medical euphemisms followed, as the men in white coats belatedly sensed what they were dealing with. But Gulf War syndrome wrongly implied a single war had caused it. Now we're left with the clinicians' favourite, Post-Traumatic Stress Disorder, suggesting a mild interruption in the normal swim of events, an illness that may be cured—surely the grossest understatement of our century.

The cure, however, lies deeper: in human beings, and governments, facing the truth about war and actually deciding to end it. And that is the triumph of this mighty little classic. *The Odd Angry Shot* reveals, in a mere 140-odd pages, the face of war: how it damages and destroys not only life and limb, but also the brains, hopes and dreams of everyone involved. First published in 1975, it is an Australian *Dispatches* and—like Michael Herr's classic, which came out two years later—it rips the scales from our eyes.

The Odd Angry Shot moves like a roving lens around this dreadful world, capturing a few brief months in the lives of an SAS squadron deployed to Vietnam in 1968, the year of the Tet Offensive, the bloodiest of the fifteen-year struggle. The experiences of Harry, Bung, Bill, Dawson and Rogers tell us more about the causes of war trauma than any doctor or medical analysis could. Their lives attune the reader to the reality of how men react to the dirtiest of jobs. They're cut adrift in a war their government has ordered them to join; yet they couldn't care less why, or for what purpose. And therein lies their tragedy, and ours: they are doing their duty for a nation that couldn't give a damn.

It is all so brutally honest—in the coarseness of their jokes and ribaldry, in the stench and dirt. Their lost lovers and estranged families exist somewhere in a far-off alien world called Home. We see and feel the damage being inflicted on these blokes; we sense the broken and disabused lives forming before our eyes— that is, for those of them who survive.

Having witnessed their friends' deaths—and *The Odd Angry Shot* spares no detail of the gruesome handiwork of a 'jumping jack' mine—these men grow even harder, more hate-filled. They hate the Vietnamese, the nogs—enemy or ally. They smash up one who dares try to steal from them; they push an innocent bicycle rider off the road, for a laugh; and they watch an enemy soldier roll about in white phosphorus agony before someone has the humanity to shoot him.

William Nagle knew his stuff. Himself a Vietnam veteran, he was assigned to the SAS Regiment, initially as a cook and then as a member of 3 Squadron, in Vietnam. The SAS he portrays is not the one usually described with hyperbole as the 'toughest', 'most elite', 'most secretive' unit in the Australian armed forces, whose big laconic heroes casually cheat death when not administering aid to the natives.

The SAS may be all these things; but it is also something else. In 'Nam they were in the business of ratcheting up the infantry's body counts, usually through lethal ambushes. The soldiers of one SAS unit in Vietnam celebrated reaching their first hundred 'kills' with a barbecue. And why not? It was a war.

That was their job. They were not only intelligence gatherers; they were hunter-killers. So afraid were the enemy of the SAS they dubbed them *ma rung*—phantoms of the jungle—and put a heavy price on their heads. There is a desperate irony in the fact that in 1968 the North Vietnamese, at least, respected them.

If these men were the best trained killers in Australia, they were also the brightest—the thinking man's thug—and *The Odd Angry Shot* presents their war through a professional's prism. The SAS trooper scorns higher rank in other units, because he can; he doesn't play by the infantryman's rules. He does as he chooses. During range practice, for example, the men shoot up a large water drum, clearly not a target:

The drum leaps into the air and slams into the sandbags that line the range wall.

'Drinks for my friends [the insects],' grins Bung, removing the magazine from his rifle.

Predictably, we are soon joined by an enraged range supervisor.

'Weel,' screams the corporal...'what smart prick did that?'...

'Fucked if I know, mate,' answers Rogers, wiping the dust cover of his rifle...

'Must've been a ricochet,' says Bung, looking innocently at the furious NCO.

And the SAS trooper remembers. The repetition of that word 'remember' haunts the text like a recurrent curse: remember the losses; remember your dead friend; remember his guts spilled on the road; remember the baying protestors; remember the deceit and hypocrisy of politicians. Let this book again be a warning to all those newly minted warmongers, Anzac Day zealots, hero-hunting journalists and populist storytellers posing as historians who seem to have forgotten what war is and does. The fallen deserve to be commemorated—but we must first *remember* them, and what actually happens in a war. Lest we forget.

Nagle was charged and punished for refusing to cook egg custard. It must have been a very funny act of defiance. His humour is born of darkness; in places this book is the blackest of black comedies, as if some malevolent spirit had dropped the men into a lower circle of hell and they survive by laughing at it. The duel between Bung's pet spider and a sapper's scorpion is funny because the insects have as little hope as their owners.

Yet *The Odd Angry Shot* is, at heart, a tragedy. The joke, ultimately, is on them—and in a wider sense, us. 'We are stuck here, refusing to admit defeat,' the narrator warns, 'an army of frustrated pawns, tired, wet and sold out...You [the politicians and the people] have lied to us for the last time. We, the survivors, will come home, will move amongst you, will wait, will be revenged.'

A page later he portrays the once-proud SAS soldier in Vietnam as 'an organ grinder's monkey dressed in green'. The identity of the organ grinder is monstrously clear.

The Odd Angry Shot

STANDING beside a forty-four gallon drum filled with coke at the airbase. Richmond, wasn't it?

Shit it's cold. Pissing rain. Remember how your back froze when you turned around and your front froze when you did the reverse.

Harry arrived with two cups of cocoa made on milk.

'You know we're getting Armalites when we get there.'

'What, straight away?'

'No. When we get to Nui Dat.'

'Shit, we'll stir the indigenous population up then, eh?'

'Remember what the man said: "You are visitors in South Vietnam,"' said Harry.

'Thank the Jesus that it's over there and not here.'

'What d'you mean?'

'That we're visitors.'

Remember Smokie Dawson on the other side of the forty-four gallon drum and the way his face seemed distorted by the heat haze.

'I can just see my old lady's face if the old moll next door came in for a natter and sprayed the lounge with 7.62 tracer.'

'It'd scare the fuck out of yer flying ducks,' said Harry.

Remember when he said that I laughed. The plastic mug warmed my hands. Harry and I were mates.

'Ready to emplane in fifteen minutes. Ready to emplane in fifteen minutes. Ready to emplane in...'

'Jesus, does he think a man's deaf, bloody RAAF pogo.' Grab your rifle boy, kiss goodbye to the southern land of the Holy Ghost—that's what they called it in grade four.

A Qantas 707. 'Shit! This is the way to go to war,' said Harry.

Sleep a little. Wake up after a short while, check my pistol. Most illegal—half the units carrying their own. Beretta 7.65 mm—just in case. Only a pro would have his own pistol. Sleep. Bye-bye kids and parks. We'll protect you.

REMEMBER the bus, chartered, seemed all a bit un-military, but what the hell anyway, your mate Charlie had come out to see you off.

'Take care of yourself, you skinny shit.'

'Make sure they're all dead when I get there.'

'Don't drink all the piss over there.'

It had dawned on you as you pulled your greatcoat collar up around your ears that you were going to war. No—it had dawned on you a few days earlier when you were slumped on your bed in Room 17 and for a moment you were scared. 'Shit,' you thought, 'you're a pro. Pro's don't get scared, and if they do they certainly don't show it.'

You remembered that someone had said that more people die in road accidents in Australia than get killed in Vietnam. That was reassuring. You told yourself that you didn't need reassuring, you were a pro—you'd jumped out of planes, climbed cliffs, had wings on your sleeve—you were better than the rest of them already; you could take it; what the hell anyway.

You hoped that the bitch who hadn't written to you for weeks would miss you when you were gone. She'd write—she'd wake up to the fact that you were a man and that you were the type of man who would look after her and protect her etc.

Remember when you got to the airport, seven days' pre-embarkation leave, that's what it said on the leave pass, you had to stand in the queue and wait to check

3

your baggage in, but you didn't. You knew that they were only civilians, and you somehow felt better than them—superior—you were protecting them. Luggage checked in. 'Go for a walk, eh?' Yeah, let's have a bit of a stroll around the place. Strain your ears when you walk past groups of people; they knew you were going to war; they knew you weren't like all these long-haired bastards; they knew that you were one of the gutsy ones, you'd lay down your life for them—and, by Jesus, for your country too—yeah, your country was important, they knew that.

Strain your ears a bit more, are they talking about us—they looked at us—shit, they might be here to see us off. Isn't that bloody nice of them, you know they're the type of Australian we're fighting for. Good on 'em. Notice a poster—WELCOME HOME ROBYN. Remember feeling like you wished that you could have taken Robyn's place—it wasn't us after all—feel a little stupid? Fuck 'em, rotten bastards, they could all drop dead right now and you wouldn't lose one ounce of sleep—wouldn't bat an eyelid.

Courage regained, you're still on top. Who the hell was Robyn anyway—your war was in the papers every day.

Bloody Robyn wasn't more important than you anyway.

THE party tonight, you weren't nineteen until Monday, but it was better to hold it tonight. It's only a day, you shrugged to your mother. Your bird had arrived—she was a bit pissed by nine o'clock—everyone was there, all of them, about eighty people. Shit! Eighty people.

'Well, a bloke *could* get his arse shot off,' ruggedly.

'Oh yes, I expect we'll see a bit of action,' nonchalantly.

'Don't worry, they'll get you, too, soon,' knowingly.

Eighty people—and the presents.

Shit, it was good of them to give you all those presents wasn't it?

Travelling cases, shaving kit in a leather folder.

Records—that's a bit impractical, but thanks, Jesus, thanks anyway.

Everyone's pissed. Some bird being groped at the top of the stairs.

You'd got yours out in the back yard—remember how you'd got her out there and grabbed her straight between the legs.

Well you had kissed her first—shit, a man didn't go the grope straight off. You were nineteen.

Remember how wet she was—that was good eh, meant she wanted it.

You'd laid her down beside the garage.

'Will someone come?'

'No.'

'Are you sure?'

'Yes. No one will come.'

Pink panties coming off. Remember finding it—the slippery, wet slit. Going in. She moaned. She's enjoying it.

'Ah, fuck me!' Moves faster. She's blown. Squeezes her thighs into you.

'Come out,' she says. Surprise, she's sucking me off. And I thought I wasn't going to get anything.

You kissed her again, went inside, no one missed you. You'd do it again later; she was staying the night anyway—enjoy yourself.

We're all singing songs. We'll drink a toast to the future. No longer will men suffer. That'll upset the neighbours.

'GET one fer me.' Yeah, you bet, mate.

Stand on the station.

'See you mate.' Remember the handshakes, the twinge when you pulled out of the station. You hung out of the window—waved—yes, keep waving. Hang on. This is it.

A curve in the line. They're gone; for twelve months they're gone. Find some comrades. What, a suitcase full of large cans? Shit, yeah, forget all that family shit; you're a pro, pro's don't have families. You are a member of the Elite Regiment of the Australian Army—you're a pro.

'Got an opener?'

REMEMBER Saigon, Jesus, Tan Son Nhut. You'd never realised just how much equipment the Yanks had.

Squat down next to the coke machine, notice the holes in the metal work, mortar shrapnel. Things go better with coke—even mortars. Packs arranged in neat lines of threes, ham steaks courtesy of Qantas for lunch.

'Christ, look at that,' says Harry.

'Where?' I'm nearly asleep. Shit, I'm thirsty.

'The Hercules.' My eyes travel onto a four-engined cargo plane. A group of Americans in fatigues are loading large plastic bags from trolleys.

'Christ, they're corpses. There must be sixty-odd in that lot.'

'Are they what I think they are?' I ask.

'Yep.'

'Jesus.'

'Plenty more where they came from.'

'Fuck,' is all I can say.

'TO Nui Dat by truck is approximately thirty minutes' ride. The highway you will be travelling on has been under Viet Cong control for the last twelve years. I want one man in each truck to act as shotgun. If we have a contact we will go into a standard vehicle ambush drill. Shotguns, keep your eyes open and don't kill any fucking villagers. On the way,' words of wisdom from the squadron sergeant major.

'Any questions?'

'Sir, how do we know the difference between villagers and Charlies?'

'When they blow yer stupid head off, does that answer your question?'

'Yessir.'

We all laughed—the sergeant major laughed too.

I am almost disappointed that no one shoots at us. Shit it feels good, the local nogs are as scared as all Christ of us.

'D'ja see the looks on their faces?'

'Really make you feel welcome, don't they.'

Remember as soon as you got there—rain. Remember how you said that you'd never seen rain like it but you got used to it after a couple of days and anyway it was good to wash in; the small waterfalls it made when it spilled down from the roof of the supply tent, much better than that chlorinated cats' piss that the sappers used to get from the well.

There were times when it was good to lie in your own little sandbagged and plastic covered world. In the afternoons, when it rained—it always rained on time.

'You could set your watch by this fucking rain,' said Harry—every day, day after day. It became a ritual after a while, remember, as soon as it would start to rain the whole troop of sixteen men would scream in unison: 'What could you set your watch by, Harry?' and Harry would scream back, 'This fucking rain.'

AND yes, there were the card games. The OC had strictly forbidden gambling in the lines, everyone from 2 IC down gambled. Pontoon, of course, and always in the supply tent where Black Ronnie, the quartermaster, ran the games, every night.

'Pay twenty.'

'Wouldn't that fuck ya; eighteen.'

'That's the third in a row.'

'You wouldn't be cheatin' your comrades in arms would you, Ronnie?'

'Who? Me? No way.'

'My arse.'

'Buy one—and another.'

'Bust me for four bucks.'

'What are you on?'

'Sixteen.'

'Sixteen and ten is twenty six.'

'Thanks, cunt.'

'You are most welcome, my boy.'

'Bets thanks, fellas.'

Every night it went on except when you were out on operations.

'Are you playing or not?'

'Buy one.'

'Shuddup. Listen.'

'What?'

'Shuddup.'

Crump, crump, crump, crump…footsteps of death.

Jesus Christ, Incoming Mortars Incoming. The clash beside the tent made you stop dead. Christ, the stink. Crump, crump, crump. Cordite. Oh shit, remember how Black Ronnie crashed forward over the table and how you froze when you saw the hole in the back of his head and how he started to vomit. Shit, oh Jesus no—and when you went to grab him, the gush of blood from his mouth that hit you full in the face—blood and vomit. 'Oh fuck,' you said. 'Ronnie,' you yelled, 'Oh Jesus.' Crump, crump—remember how you could see the grey-blue brain pulse out its last few, jerky movements, and Ronnie's eyes. One more cough, more blood. Remember how you swore that he wouldn't die and you knew damn well that you were holding a corpse and that you were standing like a fool holding him across the table under the arms while he spewed blood over the cards. Remember how you thought that the cards would get messed up.

'Bets thanks, fellas.'

Remember how the daze passed by and you pulled him onto the table, moved yourself back into life; the world was coming back now, the mess was on fire—and how you started to hear voices again.

The medic running along the road outside, his aid kit flying behind him.

'Everyone OK over here?'

'Medic!'

'On my way.'

10

'Jesus, you hit?'

'No, Ronnie's dead.'

'You OK? You sure?'

'Yeah.'

'Medic, for Christ's sake!'

'I've only got one pair of fucking legs, mate.'

'Who's that?'

'Roberts.'

'What's wrong?'

'Lost his gut. Walked straight out of the tent. Went off about two feet from him.'

'Roll him over, keep his legs down.'

Remember how he screamed.

'Oh shit, what a mess. I don't think he'll make it,' said the medic.

'Signallers have got two dead, one wounded,' someone yelled.

'What a night. Got a smoke?'

'Thanks, mate.'

The medic runs to the signal lines, past the burning mess.

'How many?'

'Two dead, one wounded.'

The signals corporal grabs the medic by the shirt. 'You sure they're dead?'

'How fucking sure would you like me to be?'

'Let him go, you stupid shit.'

'Sorry, mate.'

'Yeah, it's OK. Forget it.'

'One got it full in the face, and the other lost his chest.'

'How about the other one?'

'Over here.'

'Where's the torch?'

'Ahhh, oh shit, it hurts.'

Remember how you stood beside the medic and watched another professional whimper and you started to have doubts.

'He's OK. His thigh's ripped open.'

'Will they cut my leg off corporal?'

'Not unless they're pissed they won't, mate.'

Morphine, clamps, saline, shell dressings.

'Move him carefully, we got a live one here.'

'Do we own a piece of board or plank or something?'

'How about a rifle?'

'Great.'

The four of us watch as the medic slides the rifle under the leg.

'Stick your hand underneath and see if the muzzle is near his arse yet.'

'Yeah.'

'OK. Now lift his arse, roll it over a bit. Yeah, that's it and slide the rifle up to his hip.'

'It's there.'

'Shit hot. Right, now hang on and try not to jolt

him. One, two, three lift. OK, now gently forward to the RAP.'

Remember how it was outside the hospital that night. Some battalions had been hit a lot harder than we had. Seven land rovers full of casualties. Some were minor, some wouldn't see morning and some, like the one with both eyes gone, would still be around in the morning but wouldn't see anything.

'I'd rather be dead.' It was Harry.

'Yeah, what a shit trick,' I replied grimly.

Good on you Harry. Remember him sitting beside you in the mud.

'Were you with Ronnie?'

'Uh-huh.'

'You look as though you've been used as a tampon.'

I started to laugh.

'C'mon we'll get those clothes off you and I'll buy you a beer.'

'Buy me ten eh?'

'You're on.'

REMEMBER the mess line the morning after. Remember how Harry and I were three parts drunk.

The Officers' and Sergeants' Mess had a huge hole in the roof, the result of a direct hit last night.

'Right place, wrong time,' came from some wit farther up the mess line.

13

'What's this shit?' says Harry.

'Powdered egg.'

'You've really excelled yourself this morning, cookie.'

'You know why they call cooks fitters and turners, cookie?'

'No, why?'

'Because you fit food into pots and turn it into shit.'

A bumble of mirthful snickering and faces break into smiles.

'Up your arse,' comes the stern reply.

'Be nice, cookie, or I'll piss in your powdered egg.'

Exit Harry. Be sure to tune in again tomorrow for another episode in the continuing saga of Harry and the Baitlayer.

Remember that mail. Parks and kids, kids and parks, sleep tight but don't forget that we are protecting you all, so do please put pen to paper.

'Rogers. Small. Small. Small.'

'He writes 'em himself.'

'Shuddup. Clarke. Westfield. Shaw.'

Remember how good it was to get a letter. You never wrote too many—maybe you should have written more—but anyway it was good. What's this? Re-addressed.

Dear Sir,
We find it necessary to remind you that your account is overdue. We would be pleased if you would settle as soon as possible—amount $3.50.

'Shit, one of mine's a bill.'
'Who do you owe money to here?'
'No. Re-addressed from Australia.'
Reply:

Dear Sir,
I find it necessary to inform you that I am at
present indisposed, and what's more I don't care
a rat's arse about your $3.50.
Kind regards,
Son of Anzac.

Letter number two:

My Darling,
I'm sorry I haven't written sooner but I've been
so busy. I've just moved flats and you know what
moving's like. I must tell you something. I think it
would be a good thing if we broke it off while you
are away. I don't want you to have to worry about
me while you are over there because I'm sure that
you have enough on your mind without me there
too. Anyhow, must go.
Bye for now,
Love…Whatever. Whoever.

Reply:

I can't even remember what she looks like. Thanks
for nothing.

REMEMBER how it seemed warm and cosy inside the tent when it rained. You liked to watch the rain. Remember when you were a little boy and you used to get your arse smacked by your mother when you stayed out in it. Remember how you used to walk up and down beside the hedge and whistle 'Singing in the Rain'—it seemed like a good thing to do at the time—and you were only six. Thirteen years isn't that long.

It was good inside the tent. The sandbags looked solid, protective in their uniformity. Someone said they looked like Besser Bricks. Oh give me a slice of suburbia and a Holden.

HARRY is cleaning his AK47. Shaw and Rogers are writing letters.

'I think my feet have had the chop. Have a look at this.'

I display my feet like two red spotted candelabra in front of Shaw's face.

'Jesus, they don't look good, mate. Maybe you've got leprosy.'

My feet are OK. It's my crotch,' says Rogers.

'Yeah, we know. You can't leave it alone.'

'You may as well forget it, everyone else in the Task Force has it too.'

'What? Roger's crotch?' says Harry, 'I always thought there was a bit of poof in the boy.'

'Up your arse,' says Rogers.

'See I told you, a dead-set queen.'

'Is there something that can cure my afflicted tootsies,' I demand.

'I'm told that it helps if you piss on them,' says Harry.

'What's it do?' I enquire.

'The stink kills you and you don't have to worry,' says Shaw.

'Go and get stuffed the lot of you. I'll go and see the medic.'

'He won't do you much good,' says Harry.

'Why?'

'He's got it himself.'

'Anyone got any porno?' I ask, and fall back onto my bed.

'YOU will patrol the area from the road here—to the edge of the plantation here.'

'What's in the area?' asks Shaw.

'Mostly VC. There have been a few isolated reports and yesterday morning's briefing reported that two fresh graves have been found in the area of grid reference 261.292. Upon investigation it was found that the bodies were NVA, probably killed by Monday's air strike. There have been no contacts reported in the area for the past eight days, so either the bastards have all gone home, or they've gone underground.'

'Any reports of bunker systems or fortifications?'

'No, the only thing reported was a small camp at 260.294, no more than six or ten inhabitants. You will be instructed at 0930 hours tomorrow so be ready to move at 0800 hours on the dot.'

'Yessir, Herr Field Marshal.'

The intelligence corporal turns up his nose.

'Why the mad hurry to get us into a dead area?' asks Harry.

'Jesus only knows,' I reply.

'He's probably not too sure about it himself,' says Shaw.

'Hey, fellas,' it's the intelligence corporal again. 'Just got a signal. You'll patrol the same area but you'll now be scouting for one of the battalions. I'll brief you in half an hour.'

'That should make us look nice and obvious with seventy odd bloody nashos wandering around with us,' complains Rogers.

'It's not that bad; all the better if we run into a great mob from the opposing team, at least we'll have support. There's safety in numbers you know,' says Shaw. I think I notice a note of hope in his voice.

'My arse there's safety in numbers. Those poor bastards don't want to even hear about war. Bloody civilians in uniform.'

'It's not their fault.'

'S'pose not.'

Conversation ended. Wonder what's for lunch.

'WHO needs ammunition?' yells the supply corporal, pushing his head through the tent flap.

'The Viet Cong do,' retorts Harry.

'Don't need any, eh?'

'No thanks. We've got more things in here that go bang than they had on D Day.'

Remember how it was the same every time: rifle propped against sandbags, gleaming like a rigid snake; eight magazines, second last round tracer. Assemble your fighting belt: two HE grenades, one white phosphorus, one red smoke; one hundred and fifty spare rounds 7.62 in the middle pouches. Water bottles, magazine thirty round—stolen from the Q Store—knife. Set your watches. Pick up your rifle clip in the thirty-round magazine. One last look at your pack straps. Check your maps. Now wait.

'OK, fellas,' comes through the tent flap. 'I'll give you the info on where you are to pick up the battalion.'

Heard it all before. Grid reference 123456. Yeah, password is blah. Yeah, terrific. Piss off, will you, so we can get some sleep.

0800. The chopper lay on the Task Force LZ, looking for all the world like three huge eggs with tails and plastic eyes.

'G'day fellas. You this morning's hiking party?' We've had this chopper crew before. Good fellas.

'Yep, in the absence of Steve McQueen it looks like us.'

'OK. Pile in.'

Shaw and Rogers sit on the back bench and rest their heads on the quilted padding, legs dangling outside. My rifle feels good as it rests on my lap, oiled and shiny. Twenty-eight rounds of keep Australia free from sin and yellow bastards. Shit, I'd love a glass of Passiona.

The chopper dips forward as it leaves the ground and seems to drag its nose—almost as if it doesn't want to go. I smile at the gunner who grins and nods at me as he cocks the twin sixties. Camaraderie here, you can feel it, these RAAF blokes are OK. How come he's wearing glasses? He's got acne too.

The morning wind lashes my face as it curls around the fuselage. Small patches of fog on the ground, green pond, yellow patches on the ground appear between the fog over the highway that leads, I think, to Vung Tan. Jesus, I'd love a screw.

'Almost there. Stand by,' yells the navigator co-pilot and strokes the air with his hand indicating a patch of bamboo on the ground. Shaw moves down behind me. It looks calm enough. Turn your rifle on its side; one last look; half cock it—yep, one up the spout. The gold cartridge looks reassuring.

'Ready—go,' I scream as I leap from the skid. A sensation of falling and landing in a heap on the ground—nothing broken. My hands are covered in mud.

Confusion. Rotors are deafening. One quick wave to the pilot and the chopper lifts away, dragging its nose again. We're in business.

Shaw edges his way into the bamboo ahead, me next, then Rogers. Harry's tail-end Charlie. Peer into the growth. Starting to sweat—our clothes are drenched.

Halt, thumbs down. Jesus Christ, a contact this early in the piece. Shaw smiles back at me over his shoulder and makes the thumbs up sign. Thank Christ, it's the battalion. I feel a twinge in the pit of my stomach. Relief. Look back over my shoulder. Harry grins stupidly.

'What a ragged-arse bunch,' whispers Rogers to me.

A young second lieutenant comes forward to meet us, handshakes.

'Golonka,' he says.

'That's not the password,' says Rogers.

'That's my name, soldier.'

I grin.

'OK, sir, what's the situation?'

Golonka, who looks as if he hasn't slept for days, pulls a map, plastic covered, from his shirt pocket.

His clothes are covered with a film of red-brown mud.

'See this rise here?'

'Yep.'

'Well, we suspect that there are about twenty or thirty nogs dug in about forty or fifty yards from it, about here,' points with a grubby finger.

'VC or NVA?' asks Harry.

'Who gives a fuck what they are. They all want to kill you,' Golonka replies.

'S'pose you're right,' says Harry, resigning himself to the ninety-day-wonder's logic.

'Why not call in an air strike?' asks Shaw hopefully.

'Want to find out what they've got in there. We suspect it's weapons and food cache. Might be some documents too.'

'OK. When do you want to move out?' I ask.

'Soon as you like. You're scouting for us, you know.'

'Who's the forward scout?'

I indicate Shaw.

'OK. Let's go.' I push myself into a standing position.

SHAW is on the point. Slowly. Watch where you're walking. Don't want to blow our balls off with one of those jumping jacks do we?

Check the map, almost there.

Thumbs down. We've arrived. My lips are dry. Christ I'm thirsty.

Shaw turns, holds up five fingers, closes his fist, then five more again.

Shit, only ten. Something's wrong.

CRASH...What? Shaw starts to scream, bent double. Gutshot.

Down flat onto the mud. Raise your eyes and peer ahead into the foliage.

'Contact front,' screams Harry.

The world bursts open right in front of your face.

Shaw is still screaming—a long open-mouthed scream and his legs are moving as though he is trying to run away. Leaves, branches fall around you.

'Is it a contact or an ambush?' screams Golonka.

Rounds crack over our heads from the left hand side of the track. More wood chips fly into the air. One hits your hand, takes off a layer of skin.

'Ambush,' screams Golonka.

'See if you can get Shaw,' yells Harry.

'Cover me and don't shoot me in the arse.'

Rogers moves towards Shaw, grabs him by the collar. He's still screaming.

I can taste the sweat as it drips from my nose. Salty. I think I'm going to be sick. My stomach contracts.

'Shit. Please God, don't let me be killed.'

'Medic! Medic!' comes from behind me. Someone else has been hit.

I turn the safety catch on my rifle to full automatic and let the whole twenty-eight rounds go into the shrubs on the side of the track, golden cartridge cases fly into the air. The jerking in my hand stops suddenly. Panic. Oh Jesus. Another magazine. No time, there he goes. I catch a glimpse of black, not more than ten feet from me. New magazine. Jesus, hurry, hurry.

Click...home it goes...cock; the bolt springs forward like a dog on a leash.

Where is the bastard?

There he goes. The foresight and the black shape meet. Three round burst. He screams...got him. No, he's gone. Wounded him anyway. I can still hear him screaming.

Shaw's intestines have started to ooze out onto the track as he writhes in the mud. I am fascinated by the blue-coloured bowel, so that's what it looks like. Rogers and the medic are lying beside him. The medic's hands are covered in blood. He's trying to shovel the smashed intestines back inside with a shell dressing. I wonder how they'll get the mud out of his stomach.

We've broken contact.

'How many casualties?' yells Golonka.

'One wounded here,' yells Rogers.

Shaw is still screaming. For Christ's sake, shut up!

'Two killed, five wounded,' comes from somewhere behind me.

'Dustoff's on its way,' the radio's op says, almost inaudibly.

'Another one's snuffed it down here,' comes the voice again.

'What happened?' yells Golonka.

Hell, I wish he wouldn't keep yelling.

'Lung shot, shock killed him,' someone replies.

And at lunch on the five thousandth day of play the score is Home team eight, Visitors one.

'SHIT, that was the worst chopper ride I've ever had,' said Harry, rubbing his behind and dumping his pack on the floor.

Remember how it felt to be back in base? Safe.

Back into the tent and out of this stinking camouflage suit. Clean clothes.

'How's Shaw?'

'What happened? Gutshot eh?'

'Feel OK? Debrief in an hour.'

'You blokes like a beer?' Heads appear, asking questions.

STANDING under the shower.

'This fucking soap is making my hair fall out,' says Rogers, his face covered in lather.

'Who makes the shit anyway?'

The water feels good. It'll rain soon. The afternoon sun has taken the chill out of the water.

'I think it's a leftover lot from Belsen.'

'Who's Belsen?'

'Where's Isaacs? Hey, Isaacs. Do you realise you're probably washing with your grandmother.'

'My grandmother is in Melbourne driving a big Chevy and she wouldn't piss on you,' replies Isaacs and raises two fingers. Everyone laughs.

'I still can't do anything with my tinea,' remarks Rogers.

'Neither can I.'

'Hey Isaacs, do you know how we can cure our tinea?' I ask.

'Why don't you piss on it?'

'It seems that I've heard that somewhere before,' laughs Harry.

We all laugh. Christ, this shower's good. The mud runs off my body and disappears down the concrete drain.

Clean clothes and socks. Sit on your bed and pull your socks on. Remember when you never took any notice of changing your socks.

'How's your bird?' asks Harry.

'I think I've been given the arse,' I reply.

'That's life, mate.'

'Yep.'

'How's your wife?' I ask.

'Haven't seen her for five years,' replies Harry.

Remember how you had it all planned. What you'd

do when you got home again. You'd get yourself a new bird, a real one, no Catholic girls' school bullshit and pretence about her. You wouldn't mind if she was as poor as a church mouse. She'd have to be presentable, sure, but you'd had your fill of private school girls and upper-middle-class mothers.

No, this one would be different. You'd go to the pub with her old man now and then—hail fellow well met—and you'd sleep with her because you felt that you had done your bit and you deserved a good woman. Shit yes, you'd look after her and make sure no one ever hurt her. You'd changed. You were a man now, all grown up. Still nineteen.

Yes indeed, it'd be nice to go home. She's home, waiting there somewhere right now. Just bide your time pal, it'll happen.

Yessir, that's what we're fighting for. It's an excuse anyway.

'THE medics are running a blue-movie show tonight at ten o'clock,' comes through the tent flap, 'two bucks a head and bring your own grog.'

'Thanks mate.'

'Don't mind a bit of porno now and again,' says Harry.

'Now and again and again and again,' says Rogers.

'You are fast becoming an old perve, Harry.'

'Got a smoke anyone?'

And Harry lapses into one of his spellbinding discourses on sexual experience.

'When I was an R and R in Singapore, I ran into this pommie marine in a bar,' says Harry getting up and moving onto the sandbags, as though to take position of official storyteller.

'Anyway, this pom starts to tell me all about this knock shop that he'd been to the night before. He says that it was a room about thirty feet long and twenty feet wide, behind some pub. Five Malay dollars to get in to see the show...anyone got a smoke?'

Red and white packet sails through the air.

'Ta.' Draws the smoke in.

'Well, he said he was half-pissed anyway. So when he gets there he pays his five bucks to get in and the place is crammed full of poms and yanks and a few pogo Australians.

'Now the place has got a curtain at one end, and he thinks it's going to be the usual bird and the dog show or two lesbians or whatever. Well, out of the end of the room, from behind the curtain, comes this enormous-looking bird and she's wearing, wait for it, a top hat and stockings and suspender belt and carrying a chair. So she bows, would you believe it, bows and takes off the top hat and puts it down on the floor about ten feet away from the chair. Now get this. She takes about half a dozen eggs out of the hat and goes and sits down

28

on the chair. What do you reckon happened then?'

'Another bird came out with half a pound of bacon and a pot of tea,' says Rogers.

'Smart shit. Well, as I said, she drops down on the chair and shoves one of the googies up her fundamental orifice, takes a deep breath, goes red, lets out a yell and guess what?'

'A rooster came in and asked her to marry him,' Rogers again.

'Are you going to listen or not?'

'Yessir.'

'Well,' continues Harry, 'out pops the egg and flies straight as a die into the top hat.'

I collapse and shriek with laughter. So does Rogers.

'Are you on the level?' I ask with tears in my eyes.

'Too bloody right I am. This bloke wanted to take me to see it.'

'Did you go and have a look?' asks Rogers.

'Well, no. You see one of the bar girls grabbed me on the business about two minutes after he'd told me and I didn't get out of the bar for a day and a half.'

A medic pokes his head through the tent flaps.

'Yeah?' asks Harry.

'Your mate Shaw died in the chopper. Shock killed him.'

'Oh Jesus,' says Harry getting down and following the medic outside.

I feel like I'm six hundred years old. Jesus, I think,

this is like Russian roulette. It's got to be me, sooner or later. Christ, I don't *want* to get killed. Stuff their professionalism.

Rogers starts to speak quietly. Remember.

'One more statistic. One more ball for the uni students and all those other bastards to fire. You know, every time one of us gets brassed up all it does is give them another reason to get out and scream *Peace, Peace, Love and Brotherhood*. Try it when you haven't got the arse in your pants and no money in your pocket. See how important you are to the bastards then, eh. They wouldn't shit on you.'

Up until that moment I'd always thought of them as being quite entitled to dissent. But within thirty seconds my attitude had changed to one of passionate loathing and I wished that I could have emptied every round of ammunition in the country into them. Up until then, I'd never experienced futile rage either. How's your tinea now, Private Shaw?

THE continuing saga of Harry and the Baitlayer.

'What's this shit?'

'Sauerkraut, smart arse.'

'Aw, be nice, cookie, or I'll shove your head straight in it. No, come to think of it, it looks bad enough already.'

Ten minutes later, 'Not bad, cookie, that was almost edible.'

30

'Get fucked.'

'See you tomorrow, cookie.'

THE small marquee is crowded with troops from almost every unit in the Task Force; muffled laughter, can tops cracking.

'More smoke in here than at Joan of Arc's funeral.'

I sit between Harry and Rogers.

'Got a smoke?' asks Harry.

'No.'

'You got one?' he asks Rogers.

'Don't you ever buy any of your own?'

'Not much point when I can smoke yours.'

'S'pose you're right,' says Rogers with resignation.

An engineer taps me on the shoulder.

'Yeah?'

'When's this bloody turn supposed to start?'

'No idea, mate.'

'The films haven't arrived yet,' says a tankie leaning forward.

'They were being shown at a piss-up at the battalion. Want a can?'

'Sure,' I reply, 'thanks mate.'

The beer washes away some of the cigarette stickiness from my throat. A cheer goes up from the crowd as two infantrymen from the battalion come in carrying several cans of film and a sixteen-millimetre projector.

The first film is about two lesbian sisters. The noise increases as the positions become more insane and there are also the ever present comments on the performances and prowess of the participants.

'Shit, if she does that again, I'm going.'

'Jesus, it's me mother.'

'You could drive an APC in there.'

'It looks like six thousand coons singing Mammy.'

We walked slowly back to the tent, remember, and no one said a thing.

If there was one thing I would have traded a year of my life for that night, it would have been a woman. What we would have given for just the smell of one, to brush an erect nipple with your lips or to place your hand between a pair of female thighs or to have your eyes sting with sweat, just once.

You were nineteen and you felt eighty, remember.

There were moments when you were sure that you could hear the party, the voices, and you were still lying between the thighs of the girl in the backyard.

Fuck their war, you thought, fuck everyone at home for not being here in your place, and you put the bottle to your lips and sucked.

'FIGHT, fight, fight, fight, fight,' comes the chorus.

'Jesus, it must be a blue,' says Rogers springing from the bed.

'Come on Harry, worth a look.' I grunt, getting up half-drunk from the bed and shakily placing the bourbon bottle on the sandbags.

It is all but over when we get there. A medic has been spraying with an anti-insect fog machine and someone in one of the tents has complained. The medic has told the complainants to piss off and has collected a broken nose for his trouble. His fog machine lies on the ground and two figures in spotted clothing are helping the medic up and onto his feet.

'Now be a nice bloke and shut up about all this or by Christ you'll get more than a bloody broken nose, sonny.'

The medic protestingly shakes himself free from the two pairs of hands holding him.

'Look pal.' His eyes are watering. Blood is pouring from his nose and spreading as it hits his shirt front. 'I've been ordered to spray this area by the MO.'

'I don't give a fuck if Rima the Bird Girl told you to spray it. Grab your fucking contraption and piss off... NOW!'

The medic picks up his fog machine and traipses away. Harry and I walk back inside the tent.

'The rot's set in.'

'What do you mean?' I ask.

'I've seen it before. Got a smoke?'

'Yeah, here,' I throw the packet and it lands on the sandbags. Harry takes one and throws the packet back to me. He lights it with the communal Zippo that hangs from the roof.

'Well, first of all, when they start to argue that's bad enough. A few piss-offs and get-stuffeds and nobody really takes any notice of it. Then it gets to stage two, the camaraderie and all this esprit bullshit just goes. Then comes stage three when they start to fight with one another and the morale goes. And once the morale goes the casualties start to mount up, and the sick parades start to get larger, and all we want to do is to get the bloody job over and done with, so we don't move unless we have to and we don't take any more risks—because there's no reason to.'

'I think you've got something there. It's been going on for quite a while.'

'Right,' says Harry. Remember when he said that.

EARLY afternoon, enter one face with one worried expression. It's our old buddy Bung Holey from twenty-one patrol.

'Greetings, oh saviours of mankind and the free world,' says Bung bowing almost double.

'And much respects to you and your charming husband, your Godship, what can we do for you?' says Harry, looking up from his book.

'Ah,' says Bung trying to achieve a look of mock tragedy. 'As you are all no doubt aware, we have had occasion to use one another's equipment from time to time and so, my sons, I was wondering if you had come into contact at all with the cunt who's pinched my pack.'

'Your what?'

'My pack.'

'Where was it when you last saw it?' asks Rogers.

'Out the back on the wire fence.'

'Now,' says Harry rolling onto his feet from the side of the bed, 'it may be Bung, that we can be of service in some small way. But as you know we are businessmen.'

'Go on,' says Bung, 'there's got to be a catch.'

'I would say that it will cost you one dozen cans of the finest ale for we three to get off our arses and find your pack.'

'It's a deal. Are you sure you know where it is?'

'We are about ninety per cent sure.'

'OK. Where is it?'

'Cans first, thank you.'

Bung disappears and reappears in the space of about fifteen seconds carrying exactly one dozen cans.

'Are they cold?' asks Harry.

'Aw, for fuck's sake,' snaps Bung, 'yeah, freezing.'

'Good man,' says Harry.

I am sitting on my stretcher and watching the proceedings with open-mouthed amazement.

'Now, Bung old son, we too have been losing gear for some time and it wasn't until a few days ago that I found one of our marker panels under that large tree at the back of the lines. Now come here.' Harry and Bung walk to the back of the tent.

'Now you see where my finger is pointing?'

'Yeah.'

'*Well, in that tree is a great big fucking orang-outang and we are sure, that is I am sure, that not only is your pack there with him, but every other piece of gear that we've lost in the past week or so is there too.*'

'Well I'll be buggered,' mutters Bung, shaking his head.

'Well spoken sir,' says Rogers.

'Get stuffed.'

'Now,' says Harry again, 'we don't quite know how we're going to get our gear away from him because I'm fucking well sure that I'm not going near him, and I don't suppose that anyone else is going to have a bash at him either.'

'Why can't we shoot him?' asks Bung.

'Can't. The 2 IC knows about him and says that shooting is out of the question.'

'Why?'

'How in the Jesus would I know, maybe it's something like the bloke who shot the albatross. He just said "NO, N, O".'

'And this cost me a dozen cans?'

'We did our best, Bung. Here's half a dozen of them back.'

'Thanks, cunt.'

'LEAVE allocations are on the notice board,' says Rogers from the doorway of the tent.

'When do we go?' asks Harry.

'On the twelfth.'

'What's today?' I ask.

'Today is the...' painful calculation, 'today is the third,' replies Rogers counting on his fingers.

'Who's going?' I ask.

'You, me, Harry and Bung Holey,' he replies.

'Vung Tau?'

'Yessir.'

'I've got halfa already,' says Harry thrusting his hips forward.

THE mess line assembles for the umpteenth time. 'Where's your mate Harry?' asks the cook with a sneer. 'Recovering from a hangover, eh?'

'No. You've finally poisoned him,' replies Rogers from behind me.

The plate fills as cookie spoons chicken, potatoes, sauerkraut and sweet corn. The water from the sweet corn spills onto my fingers. I lick them as I walk towards the mess tent.

'Jesus, you don't look too good, mate.'

Clarkie, a member of fifteen patrol, is sitting looking at his food, his face showing pain.

'What's up mate?' I enquire, looking at the drawn

face beside me.

'I think I've got something wrong with my guts,' replies Clarkie.

'Like what?' I ask between mouthfuls of instant potato.

'I noticed it about two weeks ago,' says Clarkie. Jesus, he's even got black circles under his eyes.

'I went for a crap, and when I looked down I saw all these little white eggs in it.'

'Do you mind if I finish my dinner before you start to speak of your bodily malfunctions,' I sneer, adopting an offended air.

'No, go on,' says Rogers, looking morbidly interested.

'Aw, Jesus,' I say and move to the other end of the table, spooning potato all the while.

'Well, as I said, I saw all these little white eggs in it and I've been getting worse ever since.'

'Like how have you been getting worse?' asks Rogers.

'Well why in the Jesus don't you go to the RAP or an MO or someone?' I ask.

'I did. They made me shit in a thing that looked like a soap container and they said they'd let me know the results.'

'So what's the result?' asks Rogers.

'Don't know. I haven't heard a thing from them and I can hardly eat and when I do it goes straight through me. S'cuse me, I've gotta go and have a crap,' Clarkie makes for the door and disappears.

Rogers looks at me as I move back up to the head of the table, and shrugs his shoulders.

I shrug mine.

'Wonder what's for sweets?' says Rogers.

HARRY is sitting on the sandbags with a two-week-old copy of a Melbourne daily in his hands.

Rogers is sitting on the side of his stretcher captivated by the series of figures on the piece of paper in his hands.

'I should have exactly two thousand two hundred dollars when I get home.'

'That's if we don't drink it for you first,' says Harry looking up from his paper.

I leaf through the Roneo copy of a sex book entitled *She Devils* about three nymphomaniac sisters and a sadistic nun.

'What do you intend to do with your new found wealth when you return home?' asks Harry from behind his paper.

'Don't know, might buy a sports car.'

'Hard to screw in,' says Harry.

'S'pose so,' replies Rogers thoughtfully. 'Maybe I'll buy a block of land.'

'Knowing our luck, they'd probably put a road

39

right through the middle of it and give you four bob compensation,' says Harry scratching his chest.

'They can't do that can they?'

'You're too fucking right they can, mate,' says Harry, putting the paper down on the sandbags beside him. 'Got a smoke?' The packet sails through the air once more.

'What do you mean? Can they take your land off you even if you've been overseas?' asks Rogers with a look of disbelief.

'Look pal, don't get any ideas that you're anything special just because a few nogs have fired a few shots in your direction. They can do any bloody thing they like to you and you can scream your tits off and it won't do you one ounce of bloody good.'

'Aw, bullshit. I don't believe that,' says Rogers looking at me.

'He's right, mate, they can shoot you if they want to and there's not a bloody thing you can do about it.'

Harry lights another cigarette with the communal Zippo.

'Listen pal, you had better start to believe that the greater majority of the wonderful people back home couldn't give two stuffs if you lived or died. They're sitting on their arses in front of the television set right now, and I'll bet my balls that they are a damn sight more interested in *Coronation Street* than in your bloody welfare.'

'Maybe I'll buy the MG instead,' Rogers mumbles, a look of disappointment spreading across his face.

'Bet my balls the salesman takes you down.'

Rogers throws his pen at Harry.

'Bastards,' says Rogers from his pillow.

I FEEL behind me, my fingers searching for the top of the water bottle hanging from my belt. The morning sun is scorching.

Harry is about six feet in front of me, bent double over his rifle. I can feel my feet itching. I haven't taken my boots off for four days.

An ant travels down the stock of my rifle. My eyes glance from the ant to the foliage around me. The ant stops as if unsure of himself. I blink, squeeze my eyelids shut, and the sweat stings my eyes. My clothes are saturated. My left hand finds the water bottle. It feels heavy as I weigh it with my fingers.

Harry moves, then stops. I can hear them coming.

I look behind me. Rogers is taking a grenade from his belt. I look at Harry again and fit the rifle into the joint of my shoulder and chest.

Wait...wait until they are within about ten feet of us.

Harry points towards me. The sweat is still running into my eyes. Blink. I am to initiate the ambush. I slide a spare magazine under my left hand. The pistol grip of my rifle is slippery with sweat. I notice the chips and scratches on the woodwork and turn the spare magazine around to avoid the sun catching the brass cartridges packed, sardine-like, inside.

I feel as though I am about to break wind and contract my stomach muscles. I smile to myself as I think of the remarks if I did. Today's lecture will be on how to initiate an ambush by farting...

There they are, two of them. They stop. A straight line; eye, rearsight, foresight, head. The butt of the rifle nestles into my shoulder and my grubby finger curls around the gunmetal-blue trigger.

Fuck him, he's moved. No, stopped again. Another straight line. He's turned his head to the side. Now.

Eye, rearsight, foresight...profile...squeeze. BANG!

The butt jerks back into my shoulder. I fire into him twice more. He falls, spinning around. His companion drops to the ground and fires a wild shot over my head.

Harry's first short burst missed him. He springs to his feet and I see the look of sheer terror on his face. Harry's rifle drifts through the air and jerks as the hard nosed projectiles stitch the youth from shoulder to knee. Pieces of his equipment fly into the air as Harry hoses his body with another long burst.

We wait, then, cat-like, we move forward towards the two corpses. Harry rolls mine over with the tip of his boot.

'This one's no worry,' says Harry, now on his

knees and searching the body for documents.

The other one still twitches occasionally as if refusing to die. He will die, though. Harry's shots have taken his right side and arm off.

I look towards the signaller, now crouched beside Rogers.

'Get the choppers in. Safe extraction.'

We sit in the clearing, still peering into the foliage. The signaller is talking to the chopper pilot.

'I see smoke, over.'

'I see green, over.'

'Green, correct out.'

'Wonder what it'd be like if they had air support?' Rogers says, as the chopper hangs in the air above us.

'Thank the sweet Jesus they haven't,' replies Harry.

'WHERE do we change our money?' asks Harry of the service corps warrant officer with the huge beer paunch.

'Where do we change money, sir?' he replies.

'Do beg my pardon,' says Harry shuffling to what could only be termed as two per cent of the regulation position of attention. 'Where do we change our money, SIR?'

'That's bloody better. You blokes think you can come down here and take the fucking place over, just because you've done a bit of time in the scrub. Well you fucking well can't, and what's more you can behave like bloody soldiers while you're here. You understand that? It's no fucking picnic down here you know.'

'Yessir,' I answer, trying not to laugh.

'What unit are you from?' he demands.

We tell him.

'Ah. You blokes think you're all fucking supermen, bloody tin heroes.'

'Ah get fucked,' says Harry.

That's done it, I think. They were last seen spending their leave in the cells building behind sandbag walls.

'What!' screams fatguts in amazement, drawing himself up to his full five four.

'I said get fucked, you great, beer-sodden bag of shit,' screams Harry in reply, looming over him menacingly.

'Right, smart arses, you're all on a charge.'

'Then you'd better make it murder, because I'm going to take your head right off, pal.'

'I'm a senior NCO don't forget,' says fatguts, now not quite sure of himself or his prospects.

'Hard luck,' mutters Harry moving towards him like a snake after a mouse.

'Right, ATTENTION!' comes from behind us. The whole group, including fatguts, snaps to attention. It must be six months since I stood to attention that fast.

From behind us appears the biggest and ugliest man I have ever seen. He wears the insignia of a lieutenant colonel on his epaulettes.

'Were you about to strike this man?' he asks

quietly, not more than two inches from Harry's face.

What man? I think.

'Ah, yessir,' replies Harry, shuffling his feet.

And may I be so rude as to enquire why you were about to strike this man?'

'Yessir.'

'Well why, soldier?'

Well sir,' begins Harry, 'we asked him where we could change our money...' and begins to explain what happened.

'You called these men what, sar-major?'

'Tin heroes,' interrupts Harry.

'Shut up, you,' snarls the colonel, still looking at fatguts. 'You three behind me piss off out of here, NOW, and if I hear one report of misbehaviour concerning any one of you, I'll have your balls mounted on my office wall, understood?'

'Yessir.'

'And I would like a few words with you if you don't mind sar-major. You three beat it.'

'Yessir,' we chorus again, and disappear down the steps of the villa.

'Well, Harry my boy,' I ask, 'where do you propose to change our money now?'

From above us we hear a voice: 'You three.' We look up, and I feel nothing but dismay as I recognise the face of the lieutenant colonel leaning over the balcony.

'Yessir?'

'You change your money at the post office on the beach. Follow the road out of town.'

'Thank you, sir,' mutters Rogers weakly.

THE post office sits squat and silvery in the small hollow between the beach and the road to Vung Tau.

'Gone to Lunch. Back at Two,' Harry reads aloud, peering at the sign on the door.

We sit on the concrete verandah and lean against the door.

'What's the time now?'

'One fifty-five,' I answered.

'Five minutes. Not long,' says Rogers.

'Best count our dough and we'll give it all in at once, eh?' I offer.

'Yeah, probably save time. That's if this post office pooftah turns up on time.'

'Think I'll have a piss,' observes Rogers, getting up and walking around to the side of the building.

'Jesus, have a look at this.'

'What?' yells Harry.

'Air conditioning. These bastards have got air conditioning. Well, I'll be buggered.' Rogers slumps down besides Harry again, muttering. 'Air conditioning. Bloody air conditioning.'

'Shit,' says Harry, 'must be a rough war down here, eh?'

'I can hear the news flash now,' says Rogers, 'armed forces radio news, da-da. Vung Tau, today. Six post office workers at the Australian Logistics base at Vung Tau died from heat exhaustion when the air conditioning failed in the early hours of this morning. Two more were reported to be in a critical condition after hearing that the ice for the beer hadn't arrived.'

'You blokes want something?' This remark from a weedy looking corporal with glasses breaks the spell.

'Yeah mate,' says Harry, getting to his feet, 'is this where we change our money?'

'You'll have to go to the other end of the hut for that. And the rank's corporal, not mate, soldier.'

'Aw Jesus no,' says Rogers, 'not two in one day.'

'The other end of the hut you say, eh corporal?'

'That's right, soldier.'

'Thanks, corporal.'

'Pimple-faced bastard,' mutters Harry.

We are almost around the corner when it happens again.

'Hey soldier!'

What bloody now? I think.

'Where's your web belt?'

'Don't own one, corporal,' I answer.

'Don't you know that ROs state that web belts, black, will be worn when on leave in the Vung Tau area?'

'No, corporal,' I answer.

47

'Well, I suggest that you acquaint yourself with routine orders quick smart. And get yourself a web belt.'

'Can I have a word with you, corporal?' asks Harry, walking back towards the weed.

'Oh Jesus no,' mutters Rogers with a dismayed look.

Harry speaks quietly with the corporal for about thirty seconds, then he and the corporal come towards me. The corporal extends his hand.

'Sorry mate, I didn't know. Have a good leave.'

'Er, thanks, er corporal,' I stammer in amazement.

'What the Christ did you say to him?' I ask Harry, while we walk towards the other end of the hut.

'I told him you were a nutcase and that the last time anyone gave you a hard time you tried to strangle him.'

'You said I was a nutcase? You great prick!'

'It got you out of the shit, didn't it?'

'I s'pose so,' I answered with resignation.

'Don't hit me, oh please don't hit me,' says Rogers, backing away from me with tears of laughter in his eyes.

'Jesus, out of all the bastards in the Task Force, how did I land you two?' I grinned at both of them. They grinned back at me. Remember.

WE stood outside the Washington Bar, just down from the market place, and the Flags—a huge sign board with the flags of all the participating nations in the war painted on it.

Past us flow a continuous stream of Vietnamese, Americans and paunchy European civilians, all sweating, all smelling. A mother is wiping her child's behind in the gutter across the street from us.

'How's that for an ad for Johnson's Baby Powder?' laughs Harry.

'You want eat?' A hand tugs at the leg of my trousers. I turn to see a toothless old crone hovering over a street cooker on which is frying the most inedible mess I've ever seen.

'You want eat? You want eat, soldier?'

'No, he doesn't want to eat a soldier,' snaps Rogers. 'Now piss off, will ya.'

'You want eat, soldier?' she whines again, ignoring Rogers and looking now at Harry.

'No! Piss off for Christ's sake. We don't want to eat, understand? No eat. PISS OFF.'

The old crone bows her head and shuffles away under her load. We go back to weighing the merits of the bars arrayed in front of us. 'Hey soldier.' We turn around. 'You get fuck, soldier,' she yells, and at the same time achieves one of the most incredible feats I have ever seen. From twenty feet away she puckers her toothless mouth and spits straight into Harry's right eye.

'Good shot, madam,' gurgles Rogers. I collapse onto the footpath shrieking with laughter.

'You fucking bitch,' screams Harry, 'and you can shut up too,' he says, looking at me. 'You've got nothing to laugh about.'

'Why?' I grin, sitting up.

'You just rolled in some dog shit,' says Rogers slowly raising his eyes towards heaven.

'Oh hell,' I moan, wiping frantically at the brown smear on my trouser leg.

And cousin Ming won the Concours d'Elegance.

REMEMBER the day when—Harry and I sat in the bar with our knees resting against the table edge. Harry raises his hand.

'Garcon,' he says, waving his hand and adopting an elegant air. 'Garcon.'

A Vietnamese teenager dressed in a Hawaiian shirt approaches us.

'Two beers, please.'

We've come a long way from the pub down by the water in Watsons Bay I think.

The teenager returns within ten seconds, carrying a tray on which rest two cans of Foster's Lager.

'Two hundred pee,' demands the teenager.

Harry peels two one-hundred pee notes from the roll in his hand. 'Bloody Foster's Lager! How come the nogs can get it and we can't?' asks Harry, a tone of amazement in his voice.

'Black market, I suppose,' is my reply, in between mouthfuls of beer.

'You like buy me Saigon tea?'

I look up from the cold top of the can, my nineteen-year-old eyes travelling and undressing the shape before me. I stare like an idiot.

'You like buy me Saigon tea?'

'Too bloody right,' I answer. The bar girl sits down squarely on my lap.

'You like buy me Saigon tea now?' I fumble like a schoolboy looking for his lunch money, for the roll of notes in my shirt pocket.

'Yeah, how much,' I ask, my face buried in the female breast in front of me. My eyes devouring, my nose smelling a woman, any woman.

If you can't be with the one you love, love the one you're with. Or so the song goes…Whatever.

'You like have fun with me later?' she asks, biting my ear.

'How about now?'

'Not now.'

'Why not?'

'You buy me drink first, you show you love me.'

'I love you already,' I say pushing her back and waving the roll of notes under her nose.

A few words with the bartender.

'OK. We go now,' she says, coming back and taking my hand.

'Meet you back here in an hour,' says Harry.

We walk towards the door.

'We get cab, we go to my house and have fun. I make you happy.'

We ride down the main street, past the flags, past the market. How simple, I think, no pretence here. No please where are you taking me tonight or what sort of car do you drive or where did you go to school. Just sex—alien sex without the trappings.

We sit on the edge of her bed. I feel ungainly. My boots, worn down at the heels, stare at me from the floor. The black shoulder holster illegally worn under my shirt, sweat stains in white salty patches on the leather.

'I like you,' she says, 'one thousand pee short time, you pay now?'

'I've got nothing but time,' I reply and peel off two thousand five hundred.

HARRY sits on the sandbags, taking five-round clips from the cotton bandolier.

'Three months to go.'

'Three months to go where?' I ask stupidly. My face is buried in the pillow.

'Three months and our time's up. All you have to do is stay alive for the next three months, and home you go.'

'Anyone want some mail?' asks Rogers, coming in and sitting on my stretcher.

'Any for me?' I ask hopefully.

'Yeah, one. One for you too, Harry.'

'Thanks.'

Tear envelope as per instructions:

My Darling,
Just a short note to let you know…

I recognise the handwriting. Thanks a million.

'Not a bad average is it, eh?'

'What,' says Harry, 'don't tell me she's finally written?'

'You wouldn't credit it, would you. After nine months, one letter,' I answer.

I don't even bother to read any further.

'Anyone going near the orderly room?' I ask.

'In about five minutes. Why?' says Harry.

'Do me a favour and pin this on the notice board, will you?'

'Ain't love grand?' laughs Rogers from behind his letter.

THE dry season has arrived. Nothing rots now. In place of the green mould there is a layer of fine red dust, churned up by the never ceasing traffic. Trucks, APCs, choppers, land rovers and feet. It mixes into a fine paste as it settles on the sweat-stained, faded clothes that we all wear. Red dust is fast becoming the colour of the Task Force coat of arms. Tinea and body odour on a field of red dust rising.

Most of us have ringworm or ringtinea as it's more correctly termed. You wash it ten times a day if you can, then you start to sweat and it starts to itch again, so you wash it again and so on and on.

'Watcha doing?' I ask.

'I'm making a present,' says Rogers.

'Who for?'

'The padre.'

The padre appears now and again, come to spread the good word and save all our souls. Your ticket to Valhalla is a padre, oh Viking warrior.

'Why?' I ask, leaning over his shoulder.

Rogers turns and faces me. 'Well, the last time he came around, he asked Harry and me why we never came to church, and super-mouth Harry, instead of coming out and saying we thought it was all bullshit...'

'Where was I?' I interrupt.

'You disappeared somewhere. You know you'd do anything to avoid the padre and his bloody free jubes. Why does he always give out jubes? If he really had our welfare at heart, he'd arrive with a case of scotch and a harlot under each arm.'

'Right,' I laugh.

'Too bloody right,' says Rogers, 'it'd go a bloody

damn sight further than bless you and jubes, I can tell you now.'

'Anyway, go on.'

'Well, like I said, instead of coming out and telling him that we don't give two stuffs for his church, Harry says that we've been spending time making something for his chapel.'

'He's got a chapel?' I ask in amazement. 'Here?'

'Too right,' answers Rogers, 'the engineers built it for him.'

'I'll be stuffed. So anyway, what are you making?'

'Well, this, as you know, is a shoe box. What I've done is cut a hole in one end, and in the other I've put this little handle that I've made from a coat hanger. Now, attached to the handle is a bunch of feathers...'

'Feathers?'

'Yeah, feathers,' replies Rogers, smiling.

'Now what you do with it is, you wait until you get an erection and then you insert it into the hole...'

'Go on,' I reply, moving closer.

'Then you start to turn the handle, the feathers do the rest, and there you have it; one fully operational wanking machine, padres, for the use of.'

'So what are we going to do with it?' I ask.

'We're going to present it to him, next time he comes to visit us.'

'This I've got to see,' I say as I walk back into the tent. I sit on my bed and am just about to lie down when I hear Rogers' voice.

'Hey, Bung me old mate, have we still got any of that blue paint?'

'A blue wanking machine for the padre?' I start to laugh, and almost make myself sick as I imagine the padre, bent double in a back corner of his chapel with his baggy shorts around his ankles and a blue-painted shoe box impaled on his erect member.

Bless me father for I have sinned—turn the handle—Hail Mary—gasp, gasp. I'm sure we're all starting to go mad. Remember.

THE APC jolts along the dirt road, stopping now and again like a large metal frog caught between jumps, with the snail's eye of its machine gun sniffing the air. I sit on the steel floor with my back against the loading ramp, the muzzle of my rifle resting against my cheek, studying Harry's boots. I feel too hot to even try brushing away the fly that crawls along my lower lip. The one-hundred-degree outside temperature is intensified all the more by the steel enclosure of the tracked vehicle that seems determined to do everything in its power to dislodge us from its belly.

Rogers wipes a droplet of perspiration from the tip of his nose and the red dust on the back of his hand mingles with the sweat, forming a muddy moustache on his top lip. The glamour has gone; no more professional gung-ho here. We have become interested only in trying to stay professionally alive.

I spread my hand over my forehead and drag it slowly down my face as if trying to squeeze every drop of perspiration from my head. My hand stops momentarily and my fingers bunch together, like the feathers in the padre's wanking machine. I gingerly feel around the grit and sweat created pustules in and around the creases at the sides of my nose. One breaks. I examine the white discharge that rests on my fingers, then wipe it on the leg of my sweat drenched trousers.

The now chipped and scarred butt of Harry's rifle is resting in the crease behind the toe of his almost worn-out boot. I notice a small rust patch on the metalwork. Rogers is trying to scratch the tinea that has crept from his foot to his ankle by inserting his knife down the inside of his boot.

'Jesus,' he says, his face screwing up with pain.

'What now?' asks Harry disinterestedly.

'I stabbed myself.'

'Stupid bastard,' says Harry from beneath closed eyelids.

The APC jerks to a halt. My head is snapped forward and then quickly back, and my eyes open as my skull smashes into the steel ramp. A sickening pain creeps down from the back of my head and my nose gushes blood.

Harry lies in an upended tangle of ammunition

cases and weapons at the front of the vehicle. Rogers lies beneath him, his face buried in a pile of spent Browning .50 calibre cases.

'Where'd you learn to drive, you stupid prick?' screams Harry at the black-clad crew commander.

'Everyone out. QUICK,' screams the black-clad figure, as the Browning starts to thud away over our heads, raining red-hot brass cases into the compartment. The ramp behind me gives way and I roll, half-crawl, slide down into the dust and run for the ditch at the roadside.

Further up the road one of the APCs is burning. I hold my green sweat rag over the end of my nose, then take it away. Still bleeding, I think, as I look down at the crimson patch on the dusty green cloth.

'Ambush?' questions Rogers.

'Think it's a mine,' comes a voice from further up the road.

'If it's a mine, what are the tankies shooting at?' yells Rogers.

'Fucked if I know,' yells someone in reply.

The shooting stops as quickly as it began. A crew member from one of the vehicles at the rear of the column, his overalls more red than black, comes and lies in the ditch beside us.

'Hit a mine,' he says blowing his nose on a dirty green rag and then stuffing it back under his pistol belt.

'Any casualties?' asks Harry, offering the crew member one of my cigarettes.

'Two dead, one wounded. A whole fucking crew gone,' hisses the crew member in reply, 'and we're short to buggery of crews.'

'What was all the shooting about?' asks Rogers.

'A couple of woodcutters started to run when the mine went up,' replies the crew member. 'We thought they were Charlies.'

'Probably were,' says Harry, inspecting the mark on his cigarette where the sweat had dripped from his nose onto the paper, 'stupid buggers.'

'Who knows?' says the crew member. 'Anyway, they're in about two hundred bits now.'

We move past the now stationary line of armoured vehicles. Harry's water bottles slap into the small of his back as he walks. The smoke from the burning vehicle drifts thinly into the air. We can smell the raw flesh of the casualties as we draw closer to the ruined metal mass lying across the road.

Two bodies lie in the red dust of the road surrounded by spreading patches of crimson. Someone throws a camouflage-pattern shelter over one and an oil-stained canvas over the other.

The wounded crew member lies in the dust about twenty feet from them. Two medics are bending over him, working frantically. I notice a crimson trail leading from the burning vehicle to where he lies in the dirt.

'Shit, he must have dragged himself over there when it went up,' says Rogers.

'Give us a hand will you, mate?' yells one of the medics, turning his head and nodding at the group of us standing at the roadside. About six of us run forward.

'How is he?' asks an Armoured Corps captain pushing between Harry and myself.

'Lost his left leg and hip,' answers the medic closest to me.

'And his balls,' says the other medic not taking his eyes off the huge burn dressings he is using to try and stem the blood flow.

'Will he make it?' asks the captain. I notice that two watery lines are drawn on his dusty face.

'Not if Jesus came down and held the saline bottle himself,' mumbles the other medic from behind clenched teeth.

The dying face; tears pouring, nose running, blood spitting. Remember when you thought, what if he does make it, what if they give him a nice new tin leg and get him on his feet again, how do you tell some randy typist that you're sorry you can't screw her because you lost your manhood on a dirty road in a place called grid reference one-eighty-three-one-nine-six? She'll look sorry in her sweet suburban way and she'll be busy the next time he asks her out:

'Sorry, I have to wash my hair,' or 'I'm having dinner with my girlfriends'...Excuses, excuses.

Half a man. And so much more of a man than any one of the smug bastards safe at home who stand in the streets and scream to stop the war. Ask *him* if he'd like to stop the war, smug bastards. At least he came. No fair weather protests for him. And you knew that every dust-covered, sweaty one of you on that road that day felt the same way...

'We've lost him,' says one of the medics, standing up and wiping the blood from his hands in a piece of burn dressing. Remember, you almost felt glad for him. In fact you did.

'TIGER beer, all the way from good old Singapore,' grunts Harry as he places the two brown cartons with the black and yellow lettering on the sandbags.

'You'll shit for a week after a night of that stuff,' comments Rogers, bending over the green packet of dehydrated chicken and rice and drooling in anticipation.

'Who cares? It's booze isn't it?' says Harry, laboriously opening one of the cartons with his bayonet. 'You don't have to have any if you don't want to. I'm sure the two of us can put a bloody big dent in it without your help.'

'Let's not be too hasty about this, now,' smiles Rogers, forgetting about the chicken and rice and moving towards the newly opened carton.

'Piss-pot,' Harry gulps, throwing a can to Rogers.

'May I?' I ask, with a look of mock supplication.

'Another piss-pot.' Harry flings the cold steel can onto my bare stomach.

'You blokes like a game?'

Bung Holey has appeared in the doorway carrying in one hand an ammunition box, the top of which has several puncture holes, and a dirty, dog-eared pack of cards in the other.

'What's in the box?' asks Harry.

'Me pet spider,' answers Bung.

'Your pet what?' I ask in amazement.

'Me pet spider. I picked him up in Baria on the laundry run.'

'Give us a look,' says Rogers following Bung to the centre of the tent.

'Who's yer tailor Bung?' asks Harry grinning.

Bung wore the most remarkable clothing that I ever saw on a soldier. His 'Anzac Gentleman's Lounge Outfit', as he was wont to call it, consisted of a pair of red felt slippers, a pair of grey-white socks, a pair of black and green spotted camouflage trousers cut down to shorts, a grey sweatshirt with 'Welcome to Bangkok' printed on the back and a white handkerchief knotted at the corners on his head.

'Stand back. He's not what you'd call friendly,' says Bung opening the box lid gently. 'There you are.'

'My sweet Jesus!' says Harry.

'Ah, shit,' says Rogers, drawing away.

Seated at the bottom of the box is the most repulsive

insect I have ever seen: about six inches across, with two half-inch white fangs and two red, beady eyes set like match heads in the squat body.

'What does he eat?' I ask.

'Meat.'

'Spiders don't eat meat,' says Harry, opening another black and yellow can.

'This one does,' says Bung, closing the lid.

'What's his name?' Rogers asks.

'Gladys Moncrieff,' answers Bung. 'Aha, I see you've got a few cans of ye olde Tiger.'

'You can smell a can of piss six miles away, can't you?' says Harry, throwing a can to Bung and looking disgusted.

'Just one of my many talents,' grins Bung, fingering the cards.

The card table and seating arrangements consist of two stretchers pulled together and four ammunition cases covered by a half shelter.

'Dollar limit, OK?' asks Bung, shuffling the cards.

'Yeah. Twenty cents minimum bet, eh?' says Harry, looking at Bung and putting a can to his mouth.

Bung slides the cards from the pack and onto the slippery green waterproof cloth.

'Buy one,' says Harry.

'One more, one more. Ratshit twenty-five.'

'Buy one,' calculating numbers in my head.

'Sit,' place the military scrip notes on the cards.

'Buy one, and another, sit,' says Rogers.

Bung turns his cards over. Six, sixteen. Draws a card from the greasy pack. Six.

'Twenty two,' yells Harry triumphantly. 'Bank loses.'

The game continues throughout most of the afternoon, and the mound of empty black and yellow cans on the dirt floor grows in size.

'I'll have to open another carton,' Harry gets up and sways towards the sandbags.

'Anyone in?' comes from outside. I turn and see two figures peering around the side of the tent. One is wearing a green sweatshirt with the letters USMC stencilled across the chest. The other is bare-chested and is wearing a shoulder holster next to his skin.

'Yeah, come in,' says Bung, nodding towards the two figures.

'Bring your gunbearer with you and mind not to scratch the piano,' grins Harry.

'Engineers,' says the one with the shoulder holster.

We introduce ourselves.

'Sit down. Like a can? Only twenty cents,' says Harry, his eyes lighting up like twin neon cash registers.

'Too right we would,' says the other one, licking his lips. He takes a small roll from his boot and peels off two grubby twenty-cent notes. The cans and money change hands.

'What can we do for you?' asks Harry. 'Or have you just come to see what life's like at the sewer end of the Task Force?'

'No way,' says shoulder holster.

'We hear you've got, or one of you blokes has got, a pet spider.'

'Me,' says Bung proudly, patting himself on the head. 'Why?'

'Well, we've got a pet scorpion over at our place and we reckon that our scorpion can beat the shit out of your pet spider,' says shoulder holster smugly.

'So?' says Bung, screwing his forehead up questioningly.

'So we want to arrange a match. Your spider against our scorpion, fifty bucks on the outcome. How about it?'

'How about side bets?' asks Harry.

'Jointly controlled?'

'Fifty-fifty on all unclaimed bets. That OK with you blokes?' says shoulder holster, looking at each of us in turn.

'Fair enough,' answers Harry.

'Now, as far as refreshments go, we've got hold of thirty dozen cans of Budweiser, and we've decided that as the CO and 2 IC are in Vung Tau for a few days next week that we'd make it a barbecue cum sports afternoon with the spider–scorpion contest as the highlight,' says shoulder holster scratching his neck.

'What about the other pigs?' asks Harry. 'Are they all going to Vung Tau too?'

'I'm the only one left,' says shoulder holster.

'You're an officer?' I ask in a tone of definite disbelief.

'Lieutenant Clifford, Royal Australian Engineers,' replies shoulder holster.

'Bullshit,' counters Bung now nursing the ammunition box in which lies our fanged contender.

'No bullshit,' shoulder holster replies and hands me his playbook. I examine the brown cover.

'Well?' says Harry.

'He's on the level,' I answer as I show him the cover on which is written in large block letters the words CLIFFORD. P. I. L. T.

'No bullshit, sir,' groans Bung raising his eyes skyward.

'OK, fellas,' says shoulder holster getting to his feet, 'see you and your mob next Wednesday around two o'clock, and don't forget to bring your spider, eh?'

'We'll be there and our spider will chew the arse right off your scorpion,' yells Bung, at the departing pair.

'All bets off if one tries to root the other,' Harry calls after them.

'It's a deal,' laughs shoulder holster as he walks out onto the road at the end of the line of tents.

'WAKE up, the padre's here. Quick, get up.'

Rogers' words reach my ears and register slowly in my alcohol-sodden brain. My eyes squint open painfully and the green shape before me gains form as the images come together.

'What's wrong?' I ask, as the throbbing pain forces me to close my eyes again.

'The padre's here, we're going to present him with his gift,' booms in my ears.

I roll onto my side and swing my legs off the side of the stretcher, levering my body into an upright position with my left arm.

'Where is he?' I ask, trying to avoid the hot morning sunlight that knifes in through the tent flap.

'Outside on the road. Harry's bringing him here now.'

My head feels as if it is about to crack in the middle. I focus on the empty rum bottle lying on the sandbags behind my head. My throat contracts. Jesus, a whole bottle, I think painfully.

With no small effort, I drag my boots on and haphazardly wrap the laces around the dust-stained canvas sides. The fawn, brown and green camouflage shirt slides onto my back, and my nostrils contract as the smell of stale perspiration rises from the garment.

I stand, swaying slightly forward, and reach for the sandbag wall to steady myself. Two painful steps and I lean my behind against the sandbags as I button the fly of the camouflage trousers.

'Christ I stink. I've been sweating alcohol for the last six, no, eight hours.'

I buckle on the belt from which hangs my heavy Browning automatic in its green canvas holster and push it down low to take the pressure from my stomach. My stomach contracts and I belch.

God, what a mess, I think surveying the pile of empty cans that litter the dirt floor. Rogers comes back in and starts to laugh.

'If you don't shut up, I'll kill you, you grinning bastard,' I say through clenched teeth, trying not to move my facial muscles at all.

'You don't look at all well,' the voice belongs to Bung, who has also started to laugh.

'Could this be the same freedom fighter that we saw last night drinking half a bottle of rum while standing on his head, in this very tent?'

'So that's how it happened?' I ask meekly.

'You were the life of the party, oh fearless leader of mine,' laughs Bung now almost in a state of hysterical collapse.

'You even let Gladys Moncrieff sit on your arm,' says Rogers still grinning.

'Who?' I ask, not fully registering, and still trying to avoid the sunlight.

'Gladys Moncrieff, my pet spider,' says Bung now squatting on the floor and holding his stomach, tears pouring from his eyes.

'Oh Jesus, no! I promise myself that I'll never touch alcohol again, never.'

Bung gets up slowly from the corner. I notice his right eyebrow with an open gash above it and that his nose is red and slightly swollen.

'How'd you do that?' I ask.

'Have a look in the mirror,' says Rogers handing me the four-inch square piece of glass.

My eyes focus on a swollen black mound with broken skin in the centre of my forehead.

'How?' I ask, feeling the spot gently.

'You and Bung had a slight disagreement last night,' says Rogers smiling.

'What about?' I ask, as Bung extends his right hand towards me.

'Don't know,' answers Rogers, 'one minute you were all sitting here playing cards and the next you and Bung were beating the hell out of each other.'

'Don't you even remember it?' says Bung.

'No, not a thing,' I answer.

'Never mind,' says Bung touching the cut on his forehead. 'What's a smack in the eye between friends?'

I follow the two of them out into the hot sunlight.

Remember when Harry said the rot had set in, remember that?

'Jesus,' is all I can say.

THE presentation goes off without a hitch. Harry does the honours.

'On behalf of ourselves and all the other unit members present, we would like to present you with this small token of our esteem, and it is with, er, profound gratitude for all the wonderful things that you have done to make our stay in this poor country just a little more enjoyable, padre.'

'Don't forget the jubes,' comes from within the dust-covered group that constitutes the audience.

'...And the jubes, padre,' says Harry handing the blue painted box to the padre.

The poor man looks ridiculous, I think as I look at him standing there with his baggy shorts and matchstick legs. The padre bows his head as if to collect his thoughts and begins to speak softly.

'Boys, this is one of the nicest moments of my life. It's not easy being a padre, trying to bring God's word to angry groups of men whose sole business is fighting wars, but I would have you understand that it's moments like these that make an outsider, and although I've been in this man's army for over fifteen years, at times I still feel an outsider, feel as though he has a place alongside you.'

'I almost feel ashamed,' whispers Rogers.

The padre bows his head again and then raises it. A broad smile creeps over his face as he speaks again.

'In closing I would just like to say that this is the

most well-constructed wanking machine I've ever seen.'

Have you ever seen twenty-five war-weary young soldiers stand as though touched with a wand and turned to stone?

'Thanks fellas. Anyone like a jube?' asks the padre, still smiling.

A ripple of laughter now rising to a roar and punctuated with shouts of:

'Good on yer padre.'

'You're OK, mate.'

'You'll do us, padre,' sweeps through the ragged looking group standing in the dust outside their canvas and sandbag homes.

Someone starts to sing 'For He's a Jolly Good Fellow'. Everyone present joins in except Rogers, who is still standing in open-mouthed shock at the padre's words.

'Have to go, fellas. God bless you,' says the padre, turning and walking away towards the road.

'WORTH a look,' whispers Bung to me as he edges through the dust to the side of the road.

'What do you think?' asks Harry, handing me the green binoculars.

'Christ knows if there's anything in there,' says Bung as I press the eyepieces to my face and peer at the ornate, overgrown structure.

Rogers arrives, lies down beside Harry and leans

71

forward in order to speak to me, turning his head on the side.

'D Company from the battalion are right behind so our arses are safe.'

Second Lieutenant Pawlicki, a platoon commander from D Company, crawls up and stops at my feet.

'What is it?' he asks, rubbing his nose with the back of his dirty hand.

'Buddhist temple. Looks as though it's deserted,' I answer.

'Feel like a look?' asks Pawlicki, almost hopefully.

'Filthy, dirty, sex-crazed man that you are,' grins Bung at the young platoon commander.

Pawlicki avoids Bung's gaze as he tries to recover his dented, twenty-one-year-old officer's pride. Bung has found a victim.

'Sir?'

'Yeah?' asks Pawlicki. 'What?'

'I think I love you, sir,' says Bung grinning like a mad cat.

'Shut up, Bung,' Harry snaps.

'Well,' says Pawlicki, 'are you going to have a look or not?'

'Why not!' I answer.

'Away you go, Bung,' says Harry and gives him a shove.

Bung slides across the dirt road like a snake, reaches the other side and rolls into the ditch leaving a small cloud of red dust in his wake. I see his hand appear, thumbs up.

Me next. I feel the rough gravel cut into my knees and palms as I slide across the road. My elbow slips from under me and my face lands in a small pothole that has been conveniently filled with dust. My left eye is full of dirt. So are my nostrils and mouth.

I reach the other side of the road and roll down beside Bung, spitting and trying to clear my nose. I up-end my water bottle, throw my head back and pour some of the contents into my eye. I blink involuntarily, my eye feels better, and I take a long pull at the water bottle, rubbing the spilt liquid over my face.

Thumbs up. Harry arrives, followed by Melford the signaller, then Pawlicki, then finally Rogers.

'We'll make for the corner of the building nearest us,' says Pawlicki, wiping his nose with his hand again.

I notice my trousers and shirt. The crawl across the road has caused the red dust to adhere to my already sweat-sodden clothes and has forced a fine layer of mud from my neck to my hips and down the side of my left leg. I glance around at the four figures lying beside me. We are all the same, covered in red mud and sweat—filthy. I feel disgusted with my appearance.

'You always wear such nice clothes.' Remember when she used to say that...If only you could smell me now, baby.

'OK. Here we go.'

Pawlicki's voice snaps me back to reality, away from the full-breasted, dark-haired girl I was with, how long ago? Five hundred years, maybe six. Remember how you stank...

'Go,' yells Pawlicki, slamming his fist into Bung's back. Bung takes off and heads straight for the corner of the building that looms and sparkles before us in the scorching morning sun. I wait until he has gone about ten feet and jerk myself into a run. The sweat pours down my face and I feel my sodden trousers cling to my legs as I tear after him. We reach the corner of the building and throw ourselves down in the dust beside the wall. Rogers is lying beside me, panting like a large dog. A trickle of saliva runs down his chin.

Bung edges his way towards the front of the building and stops at the corner. The rest of us move along behind him, half crouched, our rifle butts fitted snugly under our armpits.

We've reached the corner. I move up beside Bung.

'You ready?' he asks, grinning and trying to hide his fears.

'Why not?' I answer, terrified as I think of what may be waiting less than twelve inches from my nose.

'Go,' yells Bung and flings himself forward, covering the distance from the corner to the steps at the edge of the front porch in better than Olympic time. I roll over and swing my rifle into line with the doorway.

'Nothing,' whispers Bung.

Harry and Rogers edge past me and around and past Bung who has now lit a cigarette.

'Bugger all,' says Harry from the other side of the porch. Harry's head appears from inside the doorway.

'Nothing in here either.'

'Nothing at all?' asks Pawlicki. There is a definite note of disappointment in his voice.

'Nup. Nuffin,' says Rogers, walking out onto the porch and slipping down on the steps.

'Just a few statues of Buddha. Nothing else,' says Harry, leaning against the doorway and wiping his eyes with his hands.

'OK,' says Pawlicki, 'not much point in staying here. Move out.'

'Saved again,' says Harry.

'Yes, whatever your bloody name is, there is a Santa Claus.'

'WHO'LL give me fives the spider? Eh? Jesus, fours then. Who'll give me fours the spider?' Bung is standing on a green forty-four gallon drum screaming odds at the engineers.

'Make it tens and I'll talk to you,' a drunken engineer with a mouthful of steak sandwich and a can of beer in every pocket of his clothing screams back at Bung.

'Who let you in here, you street urchin? Begone, you wretch or I'll have you whipped,' says Bung looking straight down his nose at the engineer.

'Piss orf,' yells the engineer. He throws the remains of his steak sandwich at Bung, and then collapses against the drum.

'Drunken fool,' shrieks Bung, 'get away from the betting pavilion.' Bung is enjoying himself immensely.

The engineers have constructed an arena, consisting of a wooden floor surrounded by four large wooden planks. The bets have been duly laid. The contest is about to begin. Bung is in one corner of the arena, the engineer scorpion trainer in the other.

The master of ceremonies steps into the arena, bows to the audience and is immediately pelted with empty cans and pieces of bread. The master of ceremonies immediately retires from the arena, and stands a safe distance within the confines of the audience. He tries again.

'Quiet! Quiet! *Shuddup*, bugger you!' screams the master of ceremonies. The crowd hushes.

'Gentlemen, loose your insects.'

It's a disaster from the start for our spider. Bung, already well over his limit, tips our contender from the ammunition box and, as misfortune will have it, our Gladys lands upside down on the floor of the arena.

The scorpion, taking full advantage of our contender's plight, rushes forward and impales our Gladys with its tail. Gladys gives a few twitches and expires.

'You bloody beauty,' yells an engineer, jumping up and down and spraying those around him with the contents of his can.

Bung is heartbroken and, in a fury of disappointment, jumps straight into the arena and stamps his foot on the scorpion.

'You rotten bastard,' gurgles the scorpion trainer. He launches himself across the arena. The two are quickly separated before they can do any damage to each other. Bung is carried away screaming obscenities and the occasional 'Murderers! Unfair! Murderers!'

We sing every ribald song known both to ourselves and to the engineers, drink everything there is to drink and, having demolished the engineers' mess tent and set fire to the insect arena, stagger back across the road to our lines.

We are almost at the entrance to the tents when Harry grabs my arm.

'Look, over here,' says Harry, pointing an unsteady finger.

I focus slowly on the figure seated in the ditch at the side of the road. It's Bung. He is sitting with his head in his hands, his shoulders shaking, a piece of white paper in his hands.

'Jesus,' says Harry, shaking his head and blinking.

'What's the matter Bung?' I ask, kneeling in the dirt beside him. Bung reaches out for my arm.

Like a kid, I think as I move to squat.

'What's the trouble Bung?' asks Harry moving to Bung's side and kneeling.

Bung buries his face further between his knees and starts to sob loudly.

'Bung, for Christ's sake what's the matter?' demands Harry, taking him by the shoulders and shaking him.

'Probably lamenting his spider,' I hear Rogers crack from behind me.

I notice another figure standing about ten feet from us. My eyes peer into the darkness as I try to make out the face.

'It's the 2 IC,' says Harry as the figure approaches the little group.

'Can I have a word with you?' asks the 2 IC pointing at me. I stand and walk up out of the ditch, my hands brushing dust from the knees of my already filthy trousers.

The 2 IC turns and walks back to his former position. I follow him. He outlines the situation in a few terse sentences. Two hours ago the unit received a signal that Bung's mother and girlfriend were killed in a road accident in the early hours of yesterday morning.

'I've been keeping an eye on him, from back here,' the 2 IC says. 'Make sure he doesn't do anything stupid, eh?'

'Do you want us to pack his gear, sir?'

'Says he doesn't want to go home; wants to stay here,' answers the 2 IC. 'Look after him, eh?'

'Yessir.'

I turn and walk back towards the group on the road.

'Mother,' I mouth to Harry.

Harry slides his hands under Bung's arms and drags him to his feet.

'Take his other arm,' says Harry.

I feel the warm sweat patch under Bung's arm as the forlorn little group shuffles down past the line of tents. I turn my head and look at Harry. Harry looks at me and shrugs his shoulders. A droplet of sweat falls from the nose of the sobbing figure between us.

'WHAT'S got four legs and flies?' asks Harry, cleaning the grey skin from between his toes.

I watch the cleaning ritual. Harry does this every day. Toe jam is the backbone of the Task Force I think. Ah, slimy toe jam...the Queen has toe jam too.

'Don't you ever wash your feet?' my mother says. I am three again.

The crease created by the squeezing of the knee joint in Harry's hairy leg reminds me of female genitalia. Sniff a little, you bitch. I can smell your eagerness... Smell me, eh? I know what I'll do when I come home. You'll beg for me. Moan, eh? I'll blow right into your 'middle-class trimmed party by the swimming pool and your brother studying law' womanhood.

'I don't know,' I reply.

'Two lesbians,' smiles Harry. Back to the toe jam.

'I THINK I've got piles,' says Rogers, arising from the mound of newspapers that litters the floor beside his stretcher.

'Poofters get piles,' says Bung.

'How?' asks Rogers.

I am amazed at his innocence. How can a man whose life is centred on death be so innocent?

We are the arbiters. We are more powerful than God. We decide. Like clockwork in school: Check magazine. Sight, pull trigger. Head explodes. One more to the score for the Regiment's honour. Remember the German kids at school? What's the point? Two months to go.

'Because they root each other,' says Bung, his words punctuated by the snap as the metal top on the bourbon bottle separates.

THE land rover bounces along the road like a green-painted, four-wheel ball.

Harry's face is supported by his cigarette.

'Shit, look! A nog on a bike,' yells Rogers excitedly, waving his arms.

'Where? Where?' asks Bung, standing up and swaying against the roll of the vehicle.

'Up in front,' says Harry, lifting his foot slightly and easing the pressure on the metal accelerator.

Rogers takes a matchbox from his shirt pocket

and climbs over the low wall that separates the driving compartment from the tray of the vehicle.

'Wait until we're about two feet from him,' says Harry as the land rover draws closer to the hunched, pedalling figure with the two containers balancing on the long pole that bounces with every depression of the rider's feet on the pedals. We draw up alongside the cyclist.

'Now,' says Harry. Rogers lobs the burning match container into the rear container which immediately bursts into flame. At the same time, Bung leans far out over the side of the vehicle and swings his rifle, knocking the pole and sending the cyclist spinning down the embankment at the side of the road into the mud that waits like discoloured porridge. Harry stops the land rover and we peer at the mud-caked figure lying in the black slime.

'Flamer,' yells Rogers, grinning.

'Ho Chi Minh's a cunt,' calls Bung to the dismantled figure.

We drive on knowing full well that we have just struck another blow for the cause of world communism...

Who cares?

THE frail, grey-haired, anyone-at-home's-mother-could-look-like-her figure pounds fists into Harry's shirt front, raising small puffs of dust.

The search and clear mission is now two days old. My nose is bleeding from the heat of the afternoon sun. I lean on the muzzle of my rifle and watch the spectacle with impartial interest.

'I think she wants to fuck you, Harry,' laughs Rogers, spitting and licking his lips at the same time.

Harry raises a restraining, severe, don't-come-any-closer hand and pushes the old woman back toward the open-fronted shack that has served as her home for the past sixty years.

I jerk my rifle up and cradle it in the crook of my arm swinging the grey-blue steel finger of the barrel into line with the sobbing, screaming, ragged woman.

The old woman's eyes meet mine as she falls onto her knees and shakes her head. I walk toward her. The split flash hider of my rifle touches the woman's chin.

'Inside. Now!' I snarl.

'She thinks you're going to shoot her,' says Harry, looking as if he believes that I will.

'Get up. Move!' I am annoyed by her very existence.

Harry drags her to her feet.

'Inside. Get inside, fuck you!'

The old woman staggers a few feet and collapses again on her knees in the dirt.

'What's her trouble?' asks a passing engineer.

Harry points to the green, bullet-disembowelled figure that lies at the front of the shack, the blood patch spreading in the red dust of the road.

'That,' says Harry, nodding his head at the corpse, 'came out shooting. There were three of them.'

'Where are the other two?' asks the engineer picking his nose.

'Further up the road. Your mob's got them now,' Rogers grins, joining the group.

'Prisoners?' asks the engineer.

Harry nods.

'Why the performance then?'

'We think it's her son,' Rogers answers.

Remember.

'RANGE practice? They must be kidding,' moans Harry, peering at the notice board.

'As if a bloke doesn't get enough fucking bangs in his ears as it is,' says Bung, scratching his behind and sneering at the green-painted masonite sheet that serves as the unit information centre.

'It won't hurt you.'

'Why?'

'You're the worst fucking shot in the unit.'

'My arse I am.'

'Bloody waste of time. Just another excuse to make a man clean his rifle.'

We walk back along the road towards the tents. Harry throws a rock at the cookhouse roof.

'Why are the soldiers going to war, Grandpa?'

'Because they're too bloody stupid to do anything else, son.'

I'm nearly twenty, I think.

HARRY and Rogers are discussing food.

'Better than the shit we get here,' says Rogers.

'How can you speak of our chef's culinary prowess in that tone?'

'What chef?'

'Cookie.'

'Beg pardon sir,' says Harry, turning up his nose and prising a pebble from the tread sole of his boot with a twig.

'I like hamburgers,' says Rogers.

'You look as though you were raised on the floor of a milk bar,' grins Harry.

'No, I mean it. There's nothing better than a hamburger.'

'What? Two pieces of stale bread, a lump of greasy meat and a pile of limp lettuce.'

'Sometimes you get fresh lettuce.'

'They probably give you grass.'

'Why?'

'Because you're an animal.'

'You ought to talk. You should see the way *you* eat, and you call *me* an animal. Jesus!'

'If you reckon that paradise is a hamburger cooked

by some sweaty wog who's done nothing but fart into the oven all day, then you're an animal.'

'Speaking of wogs,' says Rogers, 'I used to root a Greek bird a few years ago.'

'So?' says Harry.

'She was the maddest root I've ever had in my life,' says Rogers, placing special emphasis on the word 'maddest'.

'She was probably the only root you've ever had in your life,' grins Harry.

'I'll tell you one thing,' says Rogers sitting up and yawning, 'Greek birds are one of the best bits of crotch a man can get hold of. I used to root this bird everywhere.'

'Everywhere?'

'Any time, any place,' says Rogers, his face a study of fond reflection.

'Where is she now?' asks Harry.

'No idea.'

'You've been sitting here telling me that this Greek bird is the best invention since canned piss and you say you don't know where she is?'

'Well the romance ended very suddenly.'

'Why?' asks Harry, looking interested.

'Her brothers sprang me one night when I was chockers outside her house, and they beat the shit out of me.'

'That's a good enough reason,' shrugs Harry.

REMEMBER, fragile girl, your promises of affection and 'Yes, I'll write a lot,' open-mouthed, wagging, aroused, tongue-in-my-ear devotion.

I am looking at the sores on my toes.

You bitch.

Bung is standing on my right, his shoulder jerking as the rifle in his hands spits 7.62 millimetre holes in the wooden, man-shaped figure that his foresight bisects.

'I told you you were the worst bloody shot in the unit,' says Harry as his left hand hooks a fresh magazine under his weapon. 'Watch this, me dears.'

Harry brings the rifle to his shoulder and, sighting quickly, sends a round into the thin wooden plank that supports his target.

'One more.'

CRACK.

Harry's second shot splinters the already weakened support and the target spins sideways into the dirt.

As one man, Rogers, Bung and I raise our weapons and within five seconds every target on the range lies flattened, the wooden supports standing like ruffled-haired, tottering drunks beside them.

Bung, still not content with having destroyed the day's range practice, swings his rifle to the left, and sends a round from the hip into the four-gallon metal water drum at the side of the range.

The drum leaps into the air and slams into the sandbags that line the range wall.

'Drinks for my friends,' grins Bung, removing the magazine from his rifle.

Predictably, we are soon joined by an enraged range supervisor.

'Weel,' screams the corporal with arms waving, 'what smart prick did that?' He points to the smashed and dripping water drum.

'Fucked if I know, mate,' answers Rogers, wiping the dust cover of his rifle with his sweat rag.

'Must have been a ricochet,' says Bung, looking innocently at the furious NCO.

'And I suppose it was a fucking ricochet that did that, too,' says the corporal, now pointing to the smashed targets, his hands shaking.

'Don't know, mate,' says Harry, turning his back on the corporal and walking from the firing mound to where our fighting belts lie in the dirt.

'Don't you, don't you fucking "mate" me, soldier,' snarls the corporal, almost running to where Harry is bending over, packing his magazines into the faded green webbing pouch.

'You're on a charge, soldier,' screams the corporal, his face now white with rage.

'What charge?' asks Harry, standing and turning to face the corporal.

'Wilful destruction of Army property.'

'Oh,' says Harry, his face expressionless.

'And that goes for you three smart bastards too,'

he says, turning and facing Rogers, Bung and myself.

'What unit are you from?'

'Artillery,' answers Bung.

'OK, let's have your names,' says the corporal pulling a spotless field note pad from his shirt pocket.

Bung rattles off a string of the most improbable names that I have ever heard. Rogers starts to laugh.

'What's so funny, pal?' asks the corporal, staring at Rogers.

'Nothing, corporal, just something I read yesterday.' Bloody liar.

'OK, laughing boy, you can take notice now that I'm going to throw the book at you four, OK?'

'Yes, corporal,' answers Rogers hoisting his rifle onto his shoulder and holding it by the barrel.

'Now piss off.'

'Yes, corporal.'

We trudge down the road towards our lines.

'What name did you give me again?' asks Harry.

'Oakover,' answers Bung.

'Any such bloke?'

'Yeah, it's the Task Force 2 IC's name,' answers Bung from behind the cigarette that hangs from his lower lip, his face a study of immobility.

'Oh Jesus,' laughs Harry. Rogers and I grin at one another.

'Who said crime doesn't pay?'

ROGERS lies in the red dirt. The remains of his lips are flecked with blood and saliva. Now and again a red-coloured bubble forms, grows and then bursts on the hole that less than five minutes ago was the side of his face. Harry is taking a morphine tube from his medical roll.

'Just hang on now pal,' says a medic, wrapping burn dressings around the red stumps that were formerly Rogers' feet.

'Dustoff's on the way,' calls the signaller.

The medic screws up his face, looks at me and shakes his head.

'No?'

'Not a hope. Shock'll kill him before they get him on the table.'

'Pig's arse,' says Harry inserting the needle at the end of the saline tube into Rogers' arm.

'I'll be surprised if he does make it,' says the medic, wrapping gauze around the quickly reddening dressings.

Rogers coughs. A clot of blood jerks from his mouth and balances on his torn bottom lip.

'Jaw's broken too,' says the medic. 'See if you can stop his face bleeding.'

Harry probes the huge gash in Rogers' face, looking for veins, and spreads his hand, stopping the flow from the torn blood vessels with finger pressure. The disarranged red teeth grin stupidly from beneath his hand.

Rogers has his eyes glued to Harry's face.

'No more tap dancing for you, mate,' says Harry as Bung eases a shell dressing under Rogers' head, tying the long strips of gauze together on the uninjured side of our comrade's face.

The green helicopter descends, bumps up from the ground and sits flatly on its skids. The red cross under the Perspex windshield reminds me of a band-aid on the nose of a drunk.

'How bad?' yells one of the chopper medics, running towards us.

'Fucking awful,' answers the medic, still wrapping gauze around Rogers' legs.

'What happened?'

'Mine.'

The spinning rotor blades send clouds of dust into the already filthy group that occupies a few square feet of this shot to pieces country.

'What's gone?'

'Both feet and cheekbone. Smashed jaw, too.'

The stretcher party arrives and gently rolls Rogers' broken-at-both-ends body onto the green canvas.

'Keep his legs elevated. He's losing blood like hell.'

Rogers gurgles, then vomits.

'See you mate,' says Bung, running beside the stretcher to the chopper, not realising he is talking to an unconscious man. Rogers' eyes are closed.

The stretcher slides into the chopper's belly. The

green shape lifts from the ground, hovers for a minute, then swings its tail in a one-hundred-and-eighty degree arc, and disappears towards the operating theatre, twenty or more miles away.

BUNG, Harry and myself sit in the side cubicle just inside the door of the bar and watch the slim backs of the two bar girls seated on the cane stools.

'Morning shift,' says Harry, his finger pushing the ice cube that bobs in his whisky around the edge of the glass.

'What?' says Bung, his eyes closed.

'Morning shift.'

'What?'

'Forget it.'

One of the girls slides from her stool and stands facing us.

'You buy my friend and I drink?' she asks, coming over and sitting down beside Harry, her oval face smiling.

'Why not?' says Bung, opening his eyes and sitting up, his every nerve now alive at the prospect of female company.

'Bring your friend over.'

The other girl drops one foot from the rung at the base of the stool and slides the other foot down to join it on the floor. I look, close my eyes and look again in disbelief as she turns towards us.

'She's white,' says Bung from two thousand miles away.

'Half French, half Chinese,' she says, sitting down beside me and reaching for the packet of cigarettes on the table. Bung and I fumble in our pockets for our lighters, each trying to light her cigarette before the other.

'Where from?' asks Bung, leaning forward, almost climbing over me.

'Saigon,' answers the most beautiful girl in the world.

'My father he soldier. French.'

I slide an arm around her waist. She takes my hand and returns it to its former position on the table.

'You are very beautiful,' says Bung, desperately searching for an eloquence of praise that none of us possesses.

'Thank you.'

'Like a drink?' I ask.

'Too early,' she replies.

'What? No Saigon tea?' Bung asks in amazement, still trying to climb over my head.

'You can buy me coke.'

Bung and I dive our hands into our shirt pockets, our fingers groping frantically for the rolls of paper money that lie there. Our hands hit the table as one.

Bung and I look at one another. Remember the 'You bastard' look on Bung's face.

'I get drinks,' says the girl, standing and smoothing the front of her baggy white trousers. 'You like whisky?'

'Yeah! Doubles please,' answers Bung.

Harry, wearing one of the most astonished looks I have ever seen hold a face together, turns his eyes from the neck of the girl seated beside him and stares at Bung.

'What did you say?' asks Harry.

'When?' asks Bung, his eyes fixed on the wiggling 'You can't afford me; officers only' arse, that snaps tauntingly by as she walks to the bar.

'You said "please".'

'What?' ignoring Harry's gaze, his eyes now climbing through the jungles of imaginary pubic hair.

'You said "please". Are you bloody deaf?'

'No,' says Bung, looking as if he is seated with his feet up in the girl's vagina and thumbing his nose at me.

'I haven't heard him say "please" since we got here,' says Harry, now returning his eyes to the small, teenage breasts of his girl.

'Well, who's going to have her?' I ask, looking straight at Bung.

'Both of us?' suggests Bung, drooling.

'Not much chance of that,' I answer.

Harry, overhearing the conversation, reaches for the cigarette packet on the table, taps out three cigarettes from it and drops his hands below the level of the table. He raises them with the three cigarettes spread like peacock's feathers in his fingers.

'Short one wins,' he says, extending his arm towards me.

'After you,' I say, grinning at Bung.

'OK.'

Bung draws the cigarette from between Harry's fingers.

'Bad luck,' says Harry, shaking his head at Bung.

I screw my nose up and sneer triumphantly at Bung.

'It just goes to show, you don't have to be dead to be stiff, eh?'

'Get stuffed,' sneers Bung right back at me.

The girl returns to the table. I notice that there are only four drinks on the tray.

'Where's yours?' I ask.

'No time now, must go to work,' answers the girl, running her fingers along my epaulette and smiling. 'Good to meet all of you. Goodbye.'

She smiles, nods her head first to Bung, then myself, bids her girlfriend good-day, turns and walks out into the street.

'My friend, she teach at school,' says the bar girl, her head framed against Harry's green cotton shoulder.

Bung falls forward onto the table hitting his head and roaring with laughter.

'Six thousand harlots in this bloody town, and we land a fucking schoolteacher,' laughs Bung, his face still resting on the table. 'Let's go find ourselves another bar, eh?' He punches me on the shoulder.

'Couldn't do any worse.'

'One and one are two, two and two are four, three and three...' laughs Harry from behind me as we walk towards the sunlit doorway.

'Get stuffed,' I snarl.

As we reach the footpath, Bung breaks into a rough soft shoe and starts to sing, 'Got an apple for the teacher...' bouncing from side to side on his filthy combat boots.

'And you can tell Margot Fonteyn over there to get stuffed too,' I snarl again, standing with hands on hips and looking at Harry.

'I'll tell you one thing,' says Bung, walking up and offering me a cigarette.

'What's that?' I ask, accepting his offer.

'I never had a schoolteacher who looked like that.'

'Neither did he,' says Harry pointing at me and grinning.

THE morning passed, the three of us, now on the downhill side of sober, sway up the lane towards the ramshackle building at the end of the notorious off limits walkway known to every soldier in Three Corps area as Hundred Pee Alley.

An ugly ageing Mama San sits in the doorway.

'What you want?'

'A fuck, my dear. Three in fact.'

'You pay now. Three hundred pee.'

Hands reach into pockets and count crumpled paper into the old woman's hands.

'You want girls?'

'What?'

'You want girls? Maybe you want boys?'

'Shit, no. Just girls.'

'OK. You go inside. You wait.'

We wait for about a minute and watch as the six young Vietnamese prostitutes parade before us.

'You like me?'

'Yeah.'

'You come with me, we go make love.'

Make love? Here you go again; this is love? OK. If this is love, grab yourself a slice and run.

'You clean?' she asks.

'Like Snow White's bum.'

'What?'

'Never mind.'

'You like me.'

'Yeah.'

'Oh, you big.'

'I'll bet you say that to all the heroes.'

'Come, we lie down.'

'No. Let's stand,' I say, feeling antagonistic.

'You mad?'

'Probably.'

And at five o'clock in South Yarra, wearing white, Miss Penelope 'What sort of car do *you* drive?' is selling out for a slightly higher figure and a bouquet of frangipani.

'YOU want change money? *Ucdai loi?*'

'Fuck off, slope head.'

'You got US green? You want change?'

'Oh yeah.'

'How much you got?'

'Ten.'

'Give you three to one. You change now?'

Harry pulls his wallet out from his back pocket and slides the green and white note from the unzipped money compartment. The short Vietnamese youth takes the note from Harry's extended hand and pushes a thin roll of Vietnamese currency into Harry's palm. As Harry begins to unroll the small wad, the youth pushes him aside and runs down the street, weaving through the crowd.

'Newspaper, the cunt,' screams Harry.

'Grab that bastard,' calls Bung to two black American marines standing on the street corner.

The inside marine extends his hand as the youth runs past, grabbing the squealing Vietnamese by the arm.

'You want this slope, man?' asks the huge, green-clad black man, walking towards us with the wriggling youth in his vice-like right hand.

'Too bloody right we do,' says Bung.

'Why, man?'

'The little prick changed our money and slipped us a roll of newspaper,' answers Harry.

'Shit, that's the oldest con there is.' The marine looks at the cowering Vietnamese.

'Split fifty-fifty on all he's got,' says the other marine, 'OK?'

'Right,' says Harry, 'fifty-fifty.'

'Into the alley up here,' says the first marine pointing to a thin space between buildings about thirty feet from us.

The marine pushes the terrified youth against the brick wall of the alley, banging the Viet's head against the rock-hard surface.

'OK, sonny. Now we're gonna teach you all about the evils of robbing poor soldiers. You gentlemen may have first pitch.'

Harry crashes his fist into the squat face and at the same time brings his knee up into the youth's groin.

We take turns, not saying a word. As each one beats the youth to the ground, the next one lifts him up and continues to rain punches and kicks into the screaming figure.

Harry rolls the youth over, face up.

'Maybe we've killed him,' says Bung.

'Nah, still lots of life in the bastard,' says Harry, kneeling beside the groaning shape.

'What's he got on him?' asks the marine.

Harry produces four, neatly rolled, three-inch thick wads from the bloodied figure's pockets.

'The little cunt's loaded,' says Bung, taking the money from Harry and handing it to the second marine.

'Jesus H. Christ! Will you look at this,' says the first marine, grinning.

'OK, boys,' says Harry. 'Let's go have a drink and split this up, eh?'

'Them's the nicest words I've heard since I've been in this country,' laughs the first marine blowing on his knuckles.

'One for luck,' smiles Harry and, turning, sends the toe of his boot into the youth's face.

BUNG sits dwarf-like beside the two huge marines. Harry and I sit facing them across the table.

'Five hundred and two dollars, no cents.'

'Not bad for a night's work, eh?' smiles Harry.

'Cheers, boys,' says the first marine, raising his glass and nodding to each of us in turn.

'Want to split now?' asks Bung. 'Fifty-fifty.'

'I got a better idea,' says the second marine,

putting his hands behind his head and leaning back against the cubicle headrest.

'What?' I ask.

'Why don't we just stay here and get ourselves a room and the best whores in the joint and have us a party. Whaddya say?'

'God bless America,' yells Bung, clapping his hands.

We all laughed, remember.

'OK. Plan of action,' says the first marine. To Harry, 'You get the room. OK?'

'OK.'

To the other marine, 'You get the booze, OK?'

'OK.'

To Bung, 'And you and I are the bank, OK?'

'OK.'

'Right. To the appointed tasks, gentlemen,' says our black organiser. We jump to our feet and disappear in four different directions.

'I WANT five girls.'

'You want how many?' asks the sixteen-year-old bellboy, looking first at my face and then my crotch, his face a picture of amazement and sly interest.

'Five.' I hold up my hand.

'All for you?'

'Jesus, no.'

'OK. Be back in one minute. You wait.'

One minute later, to the second, he reappears at the head of a line of ten girls.

'You wan pick?'

I select five girls from the line.

'OK. You pay now, three thousand five hundred each.'

'Follow me,' I reply, walking down the corridor towards the room that the second marine has just entered carrying a large carton with the words CHAMPAGNE — PRODUCT OF FRANCE printed diagonally on the side.

'The man would like to be paid,' I grin at the first marine who appears, jacket front undone, in the doorway.

'My pleasure,' answers the black man and peels note after note from the huge pile that rests in his hand.

'And five hundred for you, slipei,' as he hands the youth five one-hundred-pee notes.

'Thank you sir.'

'Yeah, go buy yourself a hat.'

The door closes on the amazed face of the Vietnamese bellboy.

'Any one of you ladies like a drink?' asks Harry raising a green bottle to his lips.

'WE want to see a Private Rogers.'

'Australian?'

'Yes, miss.'

The young American nurse walks her fingers along a pile of file index cards that sit in a green steel box on the desk at the entrance to the hospital ward.

'Bed twenty-eight, left-hand side.'

'Thank you.'

'You're welcome.'

Harry, Bung and I walk down the aisle that separates the rows of beds, our rubber-soled boots squeaking on the polished floor.

'Twenty-seven, twenty-eight,' counts Bung as we pass by the beds.

A bandaged figure lies on the bed before us. The only visible part of the face is one very alert eye, blinking.

Rogers slips his hand down to the note pad that lies beside his leg on the red-crossed sheet. We lean over the bed as he slowly begins to print the word BALLS.

'What's he mean?' asks Bung.

Rogers taps the pen point into the pad face, then points the pen in the direction of his genital region. The plastic tubes lodged in his arms look for all the world like tree branches.

'He wants to know if he's still got his balls,' says Harry.

'Well, tell him,' says Bung.

Harry bends and lifts the sheet at the side of the bed and glances underneath.

'Yep, still there,' he says, standing again.

Harry nods at Rogers.

'You'll have to go now, thanks,' says the American nurse standing beside Harry.

'How is he?' asks Bung.

'Pretty good, considering,' she answers. 'They're going to make him as good as new again.'

We walk down the white, brick-like path at the front of the hospital ward, past a sign that reads SURGICAL WARD — 96 EVAC HOSP.

'Good as new, eh?' says Harry adjusting his trousers.

'What's a foot or two between friends?'

'Twenty-four inches,' grins Bung shrugging his shoulders, 'or something like that.'

BUNG is seated on an ammunition case, his hands submerged in the muddy water that laps and splashes over the side of the fire bucket that serves as our wash trough. A pile of faded wet clothing consisting of camouflage suits, sweat rags and green handkerchiefs lies crumpled together on the small piece of plastic sheeting that serves as our laundry bag.

'Don't know why I even bother,' says Bung, his eyes fixed on the piece of wet green wool that hangs dead, fish-like, in his hands.

'Bother to do what?' asks Harry, momentarily distracted from the ten-times-read letter he is holding.

'Wash these bloody things.'

'Why?'

'Well for a start,' answers Bung, 'the only reason we wash the bloody things is to get rid of the stink, and ten minutes after you put them on again, they smell just as fucking bad.'

'Sure it's not you?' asks Harry, folding the once-white sheets of paper and carefully putting them in his shirt pocket.

'If it's me, then you've caught whatever it is too.'

'Yeah?'

'Yeah, you smell like a shithouse in a heatwave.'

'Well there's not much you can do about it, mate,' says Harry, unscrewing the top of the bourbon bottle that stands beside him on the rotting sandbags.

'I wonder if we'll stink when we get out of this place?' says Bung, now standing and dusting the seat of his trousers.

'I've got no idea,' answers Harry, taking the bottle from his lips and giving vent to a loud belch.

'I used to live in the country when I was young,' continues Bung. 'We had a nightman who'd been carting shit for twenty years and you could smell him twenty yards away even if the wind was blowing in the opposite direction.'

'How's that?' says Harry, the bottle now held between his legs.

'My father said it was because the stink had gone right into his body,' replies Bung.

'I'll be buggered. You mean a man could smell like

we do for years to come, even when he's out of this arsehole country?'

'Maybe,' says Bung, still standing sentinel-like over the wet pile of washing.

'Shit! I hope not. How'd a man go trying to get on to a bird if he smelt like we do now, back home?' demands Harry, worried. 'You'd have no bloody hope against all those sweet-smelling bastards who cover themselves in aftershave every day, I can tell you now.'

'Anyway,' says Bung, 'a lot of birds back home haven't got a great deal to rave about.'

'I wouldn't say that,' says Harry.

'Shit, I would,' says Bung.

'Well in fuck's name, tell me why?' says Harry, a look of annoyance on his face.

'OK. Prepare yourself for a lecture, my boy,' says Bung, walking over and leaning on the sandbags beside Harry. 'I'd say that women, especially in the mornings, are the most shit-awful things a man can lay his eyes on.'

'Go on,' says Harry, amazed.

'They belch and groan and fart and complain and half of them look nothing like they did the night before when you met them.'

'Yeah, I'll agree with you there,' says Harry his eyes full of interest.

'On the other hand,' says Bung, now seating himself on the sandbag wall, 'you can take a bloke, roll him in the shit, jump on his head, get him pissed and so on, then shove him under a shower, give him a bit of a scrub and nine times out of ten he'll come up good as new.'

'You're right, you know,' answers Harry thoughtfully.

'Think you'll ever get married again, Harry?' asks Bung, his eyes fixed in the dirt.

'Not much chance.'

'Why's that?'

'Well, I could say that I got married when I was too young.'

'How old were you?'

'About twenty. No, nineteen.'

'What happened, if you don't mind me asking?'

'Well I got married with the idea of settling down and looking after the woman. You know, I'd been out rooting birds since I was sixteen, and going nowhere. So I think to myself, now here's one that's different, this one I can really do the right thing by, look after and all, so after a few bust-ups and a few things like an abortion, and her going out with other fellows, we finally get down to the business of getting married. Anyway, from there on in, well from about ten months after the event, she starts to ring up now and again saying she's working late, or at a work party or something, or one of her old girlfriends is in town.'

'What, was she in and out of the cot with other fellows?'

'Don't think so, well I don't know, but I'm pretty

sure she wasn't then. It just seemed like she didn't want to be with me.'

'Shit.'

'Yeah, that's what I thought. Anyway, one weekend, she rings up on the Friday night, it was our anniversary, and says she's been invited out by some people she works with.'

'Christ, what did you do?'

'Well, I cut up rough and yelled for a while. Then I started to plead with her.'

'So what did she say?'

'She just said she'd been invited and that she wanted to go. Simple as that.'

'Didn't you ask her if you'd been invited as well?'

'Yeah, and you know what she said?'

'What?'

'She said that they weren't my sort of people and that I wasn't really the type that would fit in with them. So I hung up the phone, packed my case and put it in the wardrobe. I didn't really know if I'd leave, until she came home about three in the morning rotten drunk. Well, she just collapsed on the couch and went to sleep.'

'What did you do?'

'Well, I got dressed, took the case from the wardrobe and went and stood at the end of the couch. You know, I stood there for about an hour just looking at her and wishing she'd wake up and say that she was sorry. Anyway, she didn't. So I went up and kissed her on the forehead and told her I loved her.'

'What then?'

'I stood at the end of the couch again and told her I loved her, walked out the door, joined the army the next day and here I am.'

'Shit! What did you do for a living before you joined up?'

'I was a painter, as in pictures. I even had one or two exhibitions.'

'I'll be fucked.'

'Yeah. I was, well and truly,' says Harry sliding down from the sandbags and picking up the bundle of washing. 'Well and truly.'

THE afternoon sun is stifling. Out of the corner of my eye I am watching Harry pull small shreds of dead skin from his cracked lips.

The stagnant water, home to countless mosquitoes, sits soft and vomit-like in the bottom of the disused irrigation ditch, lapping over and seeping through the lace eyelets in our boots. A wet, sour-smelling line of thirty infantrymen.

'I'll bet the leeches are having a field day,' whispers Harry, shifting his legs and disturbing the congregation of large blue flies that have found a resting place on his ammunition pouches.

'If they bite *you* they'll end up pissed,' says Bung, his hand hooked over the shiny black butt of the M-60 that sits on its bipod like an inquisitive lizard held to its keeper by the crumpled belt-chain of linked ammunition.

'Four fucking hours we've been in this sewer,' snarls a twenty-year-old infantryman as his finger scrapes the collected dust from inside his nostrils.

'Well I hope they get this over before five o'clock. I'm taking a bird out to dinner,' cracks some wit looking at his watch, his face a study of mock annoyance.

'Bloody hard to get a taxi at this hour of night too,' he adds as an afterthought.

'Well, I don't know about you,' says Bung, 'but I think I'll go home and watch television. If I'm lucky I might even catch a war movie.'

'Shit. Can I come over?' asks the nose-picking infantryman.

'Only if you promise not to pick your nose in front of the women. They don't mind getting their gear off and a bit of perversion, but they do draw the line at nose picking.'

'OK. Can I bring my whip?' asks the nose picker.

'Now look,' says Bung,' these girls are all novice nuns on holiday and I don't want you coming over and boring them to death with dull things like whips.'

Quiet laughter passes up and down the line of ten or so within earshot of the conversation. A series of popping sounds snaps us back from the far-away mood of the hopeless discussion.

'Mortars!' screams someone farther up the soggy line of men. No sooner has he spoken than the earth around us erupts, showering us with large clumps of earth and sending waves of screaming shrapnel over our heads.

'Kiss your arse goodbye,' sneers Bung as he plunges into the foul water at the ditch bottom, dragging the machine gun after him. Its linked belt snaps down the ditch side like a length of golden intestine, following him into the slime.

A shower of water and mud, mingled with broken rifles and ripped, green-cotton-wrapped limbs, bursts into the air about thirty feet from where Bung's gun group lies half-submerged.

Then it stops. The only reminder of its savage visit is the cordite smoke that hangs in the air, and the metal-punctured bodies of the wounded.

One of the medics is dragging a casualty over the lip of the ditch, pulling the man after him by the collar. He reaches the flat ground at the ditch front and rolls the man over. A dirty green shirt is ripped from tail to neck revealing a white back spotted with small, contusion-ringed holes, from each of which runs a rivulet of blood.

'Where'd they come from?' asks an infantry sergeant, sitting bent double on the edge of the ditch, his face squeezed into a thousand pain wrinkles as he cups his shattered right elbow in his left hand, the blood plooping from the smashed joint into the dust in a tap-like stream. 'What direction?'

The distant rattle of small-arms fire cuts across the query.

'B Company have sprung a Charlie mortar platoon,' calls the signaller lying beside his radio, his ear glued to the headset.

'Must be the cunts that hit us,' says the platoon commander, standing knee deep in the slimy water, and wiping his arms with his hat.

A young infantryman, his nerves shaken to the point of no return, lies screaming on the ditch lip while two of his comrades remove the half a dozen or so blood-filled leeches that have attached themselves to the side of his face and behind his right ear.

A medic runs over to where the man lies, drops to his knees beside him and crashes an open palm into the hysterical face.

'Shut up, fuck you.'

The medic sits the now sobbing figure up and slides his arm around shuddering shoulders.

'Come on lad, you're OK.'

The man whimpers and sobs nasally as the medic drags him to his feet and offers him a canteen.

'Want a drink?'

'No...' Shaking his head.

'OK. Keep your eye on him,' to the other two.

'Dustoff's on the way,' calls the signaller again.

'How many?'

'Didn't say, sir. Just said they'd scrambled.'

'Well, we'll know soon enough. OK. We'll move back two hundred metres. On your feet.'

'Here, you want some of this shit?' Bung throws a one-hundred-round link belt to Harry.

'Have I a choice?'

'No bloody way,' answers Bung slamming the black breech cover down and covering the lead that lies there.

We walk through the dry grass to our new position.

'How's he?' asks Harry of one of the four infantry-men walking beside us. They are carrying one of the stretcher cases, face down, on a dirty green half shelter.

'Pretty good. The medic just knocked him out with a shot of morphine. He's got a nice chunk out of his arse though.'

'Jesus, this bloody thing's heavy.' Bung is sweating under the weight of the large black machine gun.

'Stop moaning, or we'll give you the radio as well,' cracks one of the stretcher party.

'Up yours.'

'I'M going to kill you,' says Harry, his face a mask of fury as he enters the tent.

'Why?'

'One of those bloody harlots that you organised for that party...'

'What party?'

'The party with the two marines in Vung Tau, you stupid shit.'

'What about the lovely ladies?'

'One of them's given me a dose.'

'Of what?' I ask, feigning innocence.

'The jack, you grinning bastard. What do you think?'

'Ah well, nothing to worry about,' says Bung, 'a few jabs in the arse and you'll be as good as new.'

'The medic's taken me off the booze for a week as well.'

'Now that's serious,' says Bung, getting up and taking a green can of fly spray from under his bed.

'Now come here, Harry my boy.'

Harry follows Bung out into the sunlight. They stop and I see Bung turn quickly and start to spray Harry with the contents of the aerosol can.

'Unclean, unclean,' shrieks Bung as Harry begins to chase him down the line of tents and out onto the road. A roar of laughter goes up from the lines as the two figures, one squirting aerosol spray over his shoulder and the other in hot pursuit of his tormentor, tear down the road, leaving a small cloud of dust behind them.

That was the start of a week of torment for Harry. Bung's new pastimes consisted of piling all of Harry's belongings on his stretcher and dragging it outside the tent with signs around it which read

PLAGUE. DO NOT APPROACH. FOUL GROUND
and anything else that his agile mind latched onto.

Finally it all became too much for Harry, and in a fit of revenge he chopped off Bung's newly acquired pet tree snake with his bayonet. Not to be outdone, Bung held a simple ceremony and then buried the rotting reptile in Harry's mattress. It stank for weeks.

'DO you suppose we're doing any good by being here?' asks Bung, his feet immersed in a violet solution of Condy's crystals.

'Not much,' answers Harry, scraping the soap from his face with the blunted razor blade, the blood flowing in small streams from the nicked heads of the sweat pimples that nestle in the crease between his neck and chin.

'Why not?' asks Bung, cupping some of the violet water in his hands and washing the lower part of his legs. 'Fucking tinea,' he adds disgustedly.

'Because when we get home, we'll be an embarrassment to all of our wonderful nation. The only bastards who'll want to know about us are the silly buggers in this man's army. Let's face it, we've got no one else.'

'You mean the whole attitude will have changed? About the war, I mean.'

'Yeah, and the fact that we didn't win it. Oh, we may have held the fort for a while, but the commos will eventually get hold of this place. It just stands to reason.'

'And what about the people back home?'

'Well, I suppose it'll just be like it's been after every other war.'

'How's that?'

'Oh, a few bods will come along and pat you on the back and tell you what a good fellow you were. That'll last about a week, and then no bastard will want to even hear about it.'

'Are you serious. Do you really think they'll treat us like that?'

'Five'll get you ten I'm serious,' answers Harry wiping the razor on a piece of green towelling. 'They'll make a big deal about it, probably even make it an election issue, and you can bet your arse that within five years, every one of us wearing a uniform from the chief of the general staff downwards will have been sold out by some sticky-fingered bloody politician.'

'Then what the fuck am I doing here?' asks Bung, a look of annoyance on his face.

'You're a soldier the same as every other silly cunt in this tossed-up, fucked-up, never-come-down land and that's why you're here; because there's no one else, and everyone's got to be somewhere. And you're here, so get used to it, pal.'

'Fucking tinea,' says Bung returning his attention to the violet liquid that laps around his feet.

The face of the platoon sergeant appears at the tent

opening. 'I just thought that you gentlemen might be interested to learn that the wharfies back home have refused to load our supply ships.'

'Nice of them, isn't it?' says Harry sitting on his stretcher and grinning at the sergeant.

'Maybe they think they're doing the right thing,' says Bung. 'After all, it is a democracy.'

'What is?'

'Australia.'

'Yeah, if you've got enough dough it is.'

'Beg pardon?'

'I said if you've got enough dough it is.'

'Why's that? What's money got to do with it?'

'OK, stupid, just take a look around the unit, better still the Task Force. How many silver-spoon types do you see here?'

'None that I know of. Even most of the officers are pretty poor, money-wise,' answers Bung, now staring at Harry.

'Right! And I'm here to tell you that you're not too bloody likely to see too many, either. It's the poor man, the shit shoveller with the arse out of his pants and two bob in his pocket that makes Australia.

'Every time the shit hits the fan there he is, standing like a fool at the recruiting office with his hand out for a rifle, while all the rich boys are hanging on waiting for a commission or for their fathers to get them into a safe job. And while you're stuck overseas with some other

116

poor bastard from the other side shooting at you, who's as scared as you are, the rich boys at home are probably down having a bit of a slum and a chop at your bird.'

Harry's speech falters for a moment. 'I didn't mean that.'

'What? Forget it,' grins Bung. 'Mess time. You going to eat?'

'Nothing else to do.'

'You may have something there,' says Bung, picking up his tin plates and following Harry out into the sunlight.

DAWN is breaking. The morning sun is starting to suck the damp out of the plantation and its occupants.

'Choppers are working overtime,' mumbles Harry, half asleep, his face hidden from view by the green mosquito net that hangs over his stretcher.

'Supply or dustoffs?' comes Bung's voice from his sandbagged corner of the world.

'Too early for the supply mob,' replies Harry, getting up and looking towards the chopper pads.

'Jesus! There must be a whole squadron parked there; all dustoffs,' a tone of amazement creeps into Harry's voice.

Bung and I join Harry at the tent entrance. The three of us stand naked in the dawn light and watch as the green machines disgorge bodies and bearers in an almost endless stream that runs from the landing area to the clearing station.

'There's more up there, too,' says Harry, squinting into the darkness at the small barely visible shapes that hang far off in the air and grow larger by the second as they draw nearer.

'Wonder who's copped it,' Bung queries.

'No idea. Thank the Jesus it's not us though,' replies Harry, now sliding into his camouflage suit and lacing his boots with a well-practised motion.

'Must be one of the battalions. There's no one else out is there?' asks Bung.

'Not that I know of. Shit, they've really taken a beating whoever they are,' says Harry, rejoining us at the tent doorway.

'Everyone up. Ready to move in fifteen minutes.' The squadron sergeant major is running along the line of tents fully dressed and carrying his rifle in his left hand. The supply corporal is following him in small-terrier fashion. 'Ammunition issue in five minutes.'

'All patrol commanders report to the orderly room in five minutes.' The sar-major disappears down the road still followed by the supply corporal.

'Oh Jesus. Here we go again,' snarls Bung wrapping his heavily laden fighting belt around his waist.

'Hope it's all over by the time we get there. I don't feel much like playing this stupid bloody game at all today,' Harry growls, slinging his belt over his shoulder and wincing as the half dozen grenades hanging there smack into his back. 'Shit, a man'll be a write-off before he even gets to the bun fight,' he adds, picking up his rifle and walking out into the early morning air.

'C'mon, oh fearless spawn of Anzac,' grins Bung, 'there's a whole big war out there just waiting for us.'

Bung and I walk down the road towards the group of men that has assembled in front of the orderly room.

'Must be a big one.'

'Yeah.'

'Either the arse has fallen out of the war or Marshal Ky's lost his dog.'

'What's the news?' asks Joey Flynn from fifteen section.

'Don't know,' I reply, 'Bung says Marshal Ky's lost his dog.'

'Probably right,' comes from behind me.

'OK. Pay attention.'

The OC is standing on an upturned supply carton, slapping his right leg with a half unfolded map.

'At 0200 hours this morning, the provincial capital, Baria, was overrun by what is believed to be the advance elements of a regular North Vietnamese force.' He unfolds the map and indicates the printed brown and black rectangle that represents the town.

'We believe, and I would add at this stage that this is still unconfirmed, that the NVA are in possession of the northern half of the town. This, as you know, incorporates the main square, the bridge and the market, so there's no use telling you that it's going to be a walkover. We'll be air lifted in as soon as the one-seventy-third and the first air cavalry's choppers have refuelled. Enemy strength on the ground and in action half an hour ago...' looks at watch, 'at 0500 was estimated at three hundred plus. They have heavy weapons in support. Any questions so far?'

'Sir?'

'Yes.'

'What about the ARVN garrison troops?'

'Funnily enough, no one seems to know where they are at the moment,' replies the OC, shrugging his shoulders.

'That'd be right too,' someone cracks from the rear of the group.

'Par for the course with them,' mumbles someone else. 'Missing, believed shit-scared.'

'OK. That's enough. Quieten down. If you can't say anything nice don't say anything at all,' grins the OC.

'You will be divided into two groups. Patrols one to twenty will travel in the one-seventy-third's choppers and their objective will be the market. Patrols twenty-one to forty will travel, needless to say, in the first air cav's choppers and their objectives are the bridge and the main square. Any questions?'

Silence, except for the shuffling of feet and the rustle of equipment.

'Right. Good luck. Oh yes, I will be in command of the operation, Captain Prowse will be in command of patrols one to twenty. Captain O'Leary will be in command of the other group. Attention.'

We stiffen to attention. Our clothes are already starting to dampen as the sweat trickles down our faces and bodies. My fighting belt is biting into my hip. The sergeant major joins the group and the OC nods in his direction.

'Your parade, sar-major.'

'Thank you, sir.'

The sar-major and the OC exchange salutes.

'OK. Now listen in. You will draw whatever ammunition you need as soon as you are dismissed. As soon as you've done that, you will assemble your patrols in single file on the road here, ready to go in ten minutes. Every fifth patrol will draw one M-60. Make sure that you all have enough water for two days. Any questions?' Silence again.

'Any money?' smiles the sar-major. 'OK. Keep your arses down and your wits about you. Good luck. Attention.' We stiffen our backs and lift our heads again, as the sar-major's eyes brush over us. 'Dismiss.'

'AND what would you like, Bung me boy,' asks the supply corporal, standing in the midst of a pile of open ammunition cases, his rifle leaning against his left leg.

'A wet cunt would be nice if you've got any,' replies Bung, raising his eyebrows.

'Yeah, we'd all like some of that. How about ammunition?'

'Oh, all right. I'll have some dry ammunition please.'

'How much would you like?'

'Two bandoliers 7.62 and two white phosphorous eggs.'

'For Christ's sake, will you get on with it and hurry up,' groans from behind me.

'Bite your arse,' replies Bung. 'Don't interrupt while I'm doing my shopping.'

The supply corporal hands Bung the two green cotton bandoliers and the two white painted grenades. Bung slips the bandoliers over his head.

'Thank you my man.'

'My pleasure. Do come again. And what would you like?'

'A plane ticket home.'

And the nonsense conversation continues as the line grows smaller.

'BUILT for speed, not for comfort,' mumbles Harry, as he seats himself beside me in the chopper's port-side doorway.

The hiss of the turbines and the thwack of the rotor blades slicing through the air sharpens my senses as Harry and myself brace ourselves and wait for the aircraft to take off.

Bung is sitting on the rear wall seat between our signaller and a member of sixteen patrol. He starts to sing: 'We'll meet again, don't know where, don't know when but I know we'll meet again some bloody day.'

We all join in, drawing a look of amazed amusement from the American chopper crew, who, judging by their expressions, obviously think that we have all gone quite mad.

The chopper lifts, dips its nose and moves forward, gaining height as it leaves the airstrip behind.

'What's the time by you?' yells Bung to the signaller, trying to make himself heard over the din of the rotors.

'What?' replies the signaller.

'The time...THE TIME,' Bung screams.

'What?'

Bung points to his wrist.

'Six fifteen,' replies the signaller.

Harry nudges me in the ribs with his elbow and points down to where the town lies spread out some fifteen hundred feet below us. I notice that small fires are burning all around the market place, at least they look like small fires from where we are. Now and again small orange flashes flare up on the ground and quickly turn into white puffs of smoke as our artillery bursts its way in short five-round patterns among the cluttered buildings. Four dustoff choppers pass us at about five hundred yards' distance. One of the medics waves to us, we wave back.

'Hope he's not looking for customers,' Harry yells.

'Morbid bastard,' I reply.

'GO.' The choppers bounce up from the ground as we pile out into the dust clouds raised by the rotor blades. Bits of dry grass and leaves swirl into the air and stick to our arms and faces. The dust is already turning to mud as it covers our clothing and bodies in a thin red film that mingles, as always, with the sweat.

We race towards the canal at the edge of the town, past a small ditch where four or five medics are bent over a line of bodies. I notice that two of the casualties are covered head to foot by a strip of canvas. A crimson stain is seeping through the cloth piece that hides the smashed head of the right-hand corpse. We arrive at the canal wall, flinging ourselves down under the protective brickwork. A burst of fire slams into the wall, ripping into the hard clay and showering us with dust and rock chips.

'This is a bit bloody hairy,' snarls Harry, his face looking screwed up and savage. 'A man could get his arse shot off very easily.'

The enemy fire, well directed and carefully aimed as always, rakes the wall again.

'OK. Let's move. Let's go, let's go,' the sar-major

is crawling past us, up towards the head of the line that has taken temporary refuge behind the wall. The signaller is crawling, edging his way along through the dust in the sar-major's wake, chattering into the headset of his radio, calling for mortar support. Almost before he finishes speaking the bombs start to burst on the enemy-held side of the canal. A stray round explodes in the canal itself. An arching wave of mud and water hovers in the air momentarily and falls like spattering excrement on top of us.

The mortar fire stops.

'See if you can make it to the other side of the road,' the sar-major calls to Bung who now heads the line. Bung starts to run. He is almost halfway across, running sideways and firing short bursts from the hip, when his feet collide with the corpse of a North Viet soldier that lies spreadeagled, its intestines coiled and broken beside it, near the far side guttering. Bung's feet slip on the still-moist gut and he falls and rolls flinging his rifle into the air, smashing his face into the bitumen roadway.

He is on his knees, shaking his head as if to try to regain his senses, crawling stupidly back out onto the road in search of his rifle when the knife-like 7.92 Spandau burst catches him full in the side of the head. I see Harry, crouched beside me, close his eyes as our old friend Bung's face explodes in a hundred, never to be assembled again, jigsaw pieces of flying bone, flesh and once never-lost-for-a-laugh grey brain. Bung's faceless corpse spins and falls backwards onto the roadway.

'You stupid cunt, Bung,' I hear Harry's voice from beside me somewhere as senses dulled.

I see the sar-major and Harry lurch forward and head for where Bung's body lies. They leap over the corpse and fling themselves down on the pavement.

'COME ON! Fuck you! MOVE!' screams the sar-major. 'We'll cover you across.'

The sar-major's rifle spits and bucks as he fires a series of short bursts at the enemy position on the fore end of the bridge.

Six of us move forward, leaping over Bung's body like lambs over a fence. We reach the other side. Miraculously, none of us is hit. Down, sight, just like we did when we were recruits. I yank back hard on the trigger, spraying the enemy position, not letting go until I see the tracer round that lies second from the bottom of the magazine turn its way from the muzzle of my rifle. Hands shove into basic pouch. Change magazines. Cock the rifle. I hear the familiar metallic slap as the bolt guides a new round into the chamber. Squeeze the trigger again. The spent cartridge cases rise in a golden arc from the right-hand side of my rifle. Stoppage. Jesus Christ, what a time to get a stoppage. Cock the rifle. Look inside the chamber. It's clear. Thank Christ it's not a jammed case. Spin the gas regulation down one notch, release the bolt, continue firing.

Remember what the man said: 'Look after your rifle and it'll look after you.'

Funny how the man never told us what to do when you trip on an enemy corpse. Well, you can't cover everything in a drill manual can you?

Harry is edging forward, the white egg-shape of a phosphorous grenade in his right hand.

'Keep firing. Cover him,' the sar-major is yelling again. I'm scared and he is starting to give me the shits...always yelling.

Harry lunges forward, runs ten or so feet and flings the grenade. Heads down, hide your faces.

The grenade explodes with a sharp, almost ridiculous, crack and a fountain of deadly white phosphorous showers onto the enemy position.

A North Viet soldier, his head on fire, runs shrieking onto the road, twisting, squirming arms flailing the air as he tries desperately to extinguish the flames.

'One for Bung,' smiles the signaller lying beside me, as he sends a burst into the screaming man's legs.

The North Viet collapses writing on the ground.

'Finish him off,' someone calls.

'Let the cunt burn,' replies the signaller, the cold smile still on his face.

The sar-major sights and puts a round into the head of the screaming enemy.

'Who's the fucking humanitarian?' grunts the signaller, changing magazines.

WE move across the bridge in single file, past the smouldering corpse. The smell of roasted flesh hangs thickly, sick-sweet, in the air as we pass the enemy gun crew, roasted, still manning their guns now damaged beyond repair by Harry's grenade.

I look behind me and see a medic cutting Bung's lower dog tag from the green cord that circles our dead comrade's throat.

My toe has cracked open again. Bloody tinea.

'How does the saying go?' asks Harry from behind me.

'What saying?'

'"You knew the job was dangerous when you took it." That saying.'

'Oh *that* saying,' I reply.

A gunship passes over our heads and makes several sweeps across the market place. Puffs of smoke drift from the electrically operated Gatling guns mounted just above its skids as it rakes the wooden buildings.

A dirty, brown-coloured dog runs past us and stops next to the North Vietnamese corpse that claimed Bung. Wagging its tail, it dips its head then races down the road and across the bridge, a length of grey intestine dangling from its mouth. No gun carriages here...and it's cheaper than Pal.

'Got a cigarette?' Harry asks, lengthening his step and moving up beside me.

I am waiting for him to mention Bung.

He takes the cigarette and falls back in behind me. He says nothing.

THE rain, the most welcome mid-morning rain, starts to splash down on the smashed town in large heavy drops, drenching and cooling friend and enemy alike. Small bursts of popping, sizzling steam rise from the charred and smouldering market place. No one relaxes.

Our tired, sweaty assault group, wet clothes hanging from our smelly bodies like soaked sheets of newspaper, lies peering into deserted and burning buildings. Seventeen patrol, struggling under the weight of their M-60 and several green-painted ammunition canisters, moves up past the three-tread concrete steps behind which Harry and myself shelter. Harry is reloading the small jewel-box-size magazines of his Armalite from several compact white cardboard packages, each stamped repetitiously with the words REMINGTON CAL .222.

'Finished,' he mutters as he shoves a fresh magazine into the open metal housing that sits like a square toothless mouth in the belly of his weapon. His index and middle fingers hook themselves over the T shape of the cocking handle and the tendons stand out in uniformly spread lines on the back of his hand as he draws the bolt back then releases his grip to let it crack hungrily forward in search of the shiny new round.

The rain, cooling and welcome half an hour ago, now becomes irritating. The whole thing has gone beyond a joke. No more warrior camaraderie now. Each of us sits and waits for the counter-attack that we know must come soon.

NO more striving to become part of the efficient professional world of the professional soldier. Fuck their professionalism. The war has been lost, we realise it at last. The politicians and we the imbecile followers, imbeciles to follow, know that we have been betrayed for a political lie. Yet we are here, we can't go home when it's over, when the protest is over or when the RSL closes.

We are stuck here, refusing to admit defeat, an army of frustrated pawns, tired, wet and sold out. Yet we still believe in our task; still, after all this, we are bound together all over the world, friend and enemy alike, the soldier, the green-clad, second-class citizen of the earth, more professional in our hopelessness than all the other professional men of the world put together.

We charge no high fees to defend a grubby street. We demand no increases in rates to make calls at night. We will arrive at any dictated hour to join in our pastime— to hunt and dispose of each other in the ultimate test of the mind, the reward of which is life for another day, another week. You have angered us, all of us, your praetorians from the red tabs downwards are angry.

You have lied to us for the last time. We, the survivors, will come home, will move amongst you, will wait, will be revenged.

'You blokes like a biscuit?' The signaller extends a hand. Harry and I take a hard slab of oatmeal from the brown paper package held between grubby wet fingers.

'Ta awfully,' comes from Harry's oatmeal-filled mouth.

STEAM rises from the road as the sun reclaims its cooling water, drying our faces and clothes. Islands appear, white-ringed salt cakes drawn on acne-covered, green-hidden backs.

'What's that place?' a finger points, sabring the air towards the yellow walled building with sepia rust bleedings smeared down its sides.

'It's the orphanage.'

'You four. Over the wall and see if it's clear.'

'Call down some artillery. Why not?'

'Might be kids in there. Can't take the chance. The newspapers would have us for breakfast if we called a fire mission on kids.'

'Don't see too many newspapermen around here.'

'Don't argue. Just do it.'

'Bugger the kids.'

Four men dive across the street. A rifle ridges two pairs of hands as a dirty boot with white worn toe leather springs up from the ground, pauses on it for a moment, then swings over the wall.

'OK.' Muffled.

The other three scramble up the yellow stone and vanish.

'Glad it's not me,' hisses Harry, blowing his nose on his fingers.

I can't be bothered answering him. Two large blue flies perform a love ritual on my left forearm. I brush them away savagely, annoyed by their presence and the possibility of their enjoyment.

Up from behind the steps and make for the next doorway. A short burst of fire, then the familiar crump of a grenade as another building is cleared and exchanges loyalties.

'How many were there?'

'Two only.' Two fingers held aloft signify the kill.

'How's your ammunition?'

'Fine, how's yours?'

'Well set up at the end of this street.' The sar-major is yelling again. 'Move out. GO.'

We run the thirty or so yards to where the street ends in a confusion of broken masonry and projectile-chiselled holes. Smoke drifts from a small crater in the road. M-60 bipods clatter to the ground, push forward, sliding into fire positions as gun crews shelter behind thirty-six-inch black barrels and chained ammunition, consoling their weapons with grunts and boot shuffles, dragged through the town by their black, reptilian protectors.

Magazines changing, hooking, pulling back and clicking home. Familiar sounds again.

A water bottle arcs up from the half-diamond sweat patch of a green back and glues itself to its supplicant's dry lips. There's a purpose for everything. Even insanity.

Scan the tread soles, the worn tread soles of combat boots, green cotton pulled lash tight over bent knees and thighs.

A pair of hands followed by a head appears at the lip of the orphanage wall.

'Seems to be clear.'

'What's in there?'

'Only a few nuns.'

'Do they screw?' comes from the cigarette-punctuated mouth of a machine gunner. A few of us laugh. Most of us don't even bother to listen.

'Sir,' the signaller is calling the sar-major.

'Yeah?'

'Sunray, sir. We're ordered back. Choppers on the way.'

The four scouting infantrymen slide back over the wall, the last one ripping his shirt on the iron railing as he drops to the roadway.

'OK. Pull back.'

'Sir?' The signaller again.

'What now?'

'Sunray's congratulations on taking the bridge.'

'My compliments to Sunray. Inform him we're moving back now.'

'Makes you wonder, doesn't it. A whole morning's work for nothing,' grunts Harry getting to his feet and blowing his nose on his fingers.

'ARE you awake?'

'Yeah.'

'You're going home.'

'What?' Sitting up.

'You're going home.'

'Who?'

'You.'

'Just me?'

'No. You and you.' The 2 IC's pointing finger sweeps, stops, hovers at Harry and myself.

'How soon can you be ready?'

'Soon as you like, sir.'

'Right. There's a Caribou to Saigon in an hour, correction, fifty minutes. Hand your weapons in as soon as possible.'

'I don't believe it...YOU FUCKING SCREAMER.' Harry is jumping up and down and yelling, shaking my hand, laughing.

A few sets of camouflage clothing thrown into

kitbags. Boots blackened...impossible to shine. Half-clean set of green fatigues. Thrown on badges. Ribbon bars pinned on shirts.

Weapons handed in. Look after your rifle, it'll look after you. Try to picture home streets, old friends, families. Be there soon.

'There's no pull-through here.' The supply corporal.

'Aw Jesus, who cares?'

'OK. Forget it. Have a good trip, you lucky bastards.'

'Yeah. Look after yourself.'

Packed, ready.

One last look around the tent. Bye Shaw, Bung, footless Rogers.

Walk down the road...

'Hey, cookie!'

'Yeah?'

'GET FUCKED.'

'You too.'

Handshakes. Harry and the cook.

'Look after yourself, cookie.'

'You too.'

HARRY and I. Sydney Airport. More handshakes.

'Wanna beer?'

'Why not?'

'When's your flight?'

'Eight tomorrow.' Climb the stairs to the bar.

Red carpets. Carpets. When was the last time...

'Two of your best beers, please.'

'You just back from Vietnam?'

'No,' answers Harry.

'Oh.' The barman moves away.

Harry and I grin at one another. Looks at his watch.

'I gotta make a telephone call.'

'See you downstairs.' And on my own, I start thinking. Now for tribute and trappings...War Service Homes and new, second-hand Holdens. All one has to do...

'Another beer?'

'Thanks.'

...is raise the deposit. Bullshit's a deposit. Festooned. Still dust carrying. Still with tinea. Open your gates. Strew my path with the roses of your admiration, and I shall strut, medals, wings, badges flailing on my trusty free gift to all the participants; Boots, General Purpose...slightly used. Smile knowingly.

Pitch your condescending change to the organ grinder's monkey dressed in his green. Well, green once. (The girl beside me at the bar is making gestures as if to advertise the fact that I stink.) And I will lick up the droplets of your pitying safety and clutch them to my inept self, and sniff the dog's arse of your offerings, and let the wash of your pious love hang about my ears as the lace curtain of my military halo.

Shake your heads and let the small change purses of your mouths, so elegantly preened and purged of all grossness, whisper and grunt platitudes.

HARRY is at the bottom of the stairs, his right foot resting on a large green kit bag.

'Well,' he asks. 'What now?'

'Let's get pissed,' I answer.

'We'll drop this shit off first.' He indicates his kit bag, 'And see if we can grab two harlots. Just for fun, eh?'

'What a nice idea,' I grin.

Back at the Watsons Bay Hotel.

'Two beers please,' says Harry. Looks at me. Lapses into fluent cliché.

'Hasn't changed a bit has it? Seems like only yesterday.' The beer drips from my chin and onto my shirt front.

'What, this joint?'

'Uh, huh.' And drains his glass.

'So here we are,' he says.

'So here we are,' I answer.

'Fuckin' terrific,' mutters Harry. Lifts his eyes skyward.

'Fuckin' terrific.'

And as he said it the rain started. We would get drenched as we climbed the hill, I thought.

Text Classics

textclassics.com.au